ASH MOUNTAIN

Fran hates Ash Mountain, and she thought she'd escaped. But her father is ill and needs care. Her relationship is over, and she hates her dead-end job in the city, anyway. She returns to her hometown to nurse her dying father, her distant teenage daughter in tow for the weekends. There, in the sleepy town of Ash Mountain, childhood memories prick at her fragile self-esteem, she falls in love for the first time, and her demanding dad tests her patience, all in the unbearable heat of an Australian summer. As old friendships and rivalries are renewed, and new ones forged, Fran's tumultuous home life is the least of her worries, when old crimes rear their heads and a devastating bushfire ravages the town and all of its inhabitants . . .

HELEN FITZGERALD

◆

ASH MOUNTAIN

Complete and Unabridged

AURORA
Leicester

First published in Great Britain in 2020 by
Orenda Books

First Aurora Edition
published 2020
by arrangement with
Orenda Books and Affirm Press

A catalogue record for this book is available
from the British Library.

ISBN 978–1–78782–474–4

Published by
Ulverscroft Limited
Anstey, Leicestershire

Set by Words & Graphics Ltd.
Anstey, Leicestershire
Printed and bound in Great Britain by
TJ Books Limited, Padstow, Cornwall

This book is printed on acid-free paper

PART ONE

THE MONUMENT

1

Monday 26th January, 3.30 pm

*'If you want Fran to die, add two. That's
zero-two if you would like to say goodbye to
Francesca.'*
Fran unstuck herself from the couch and
reached for the alarm. In the background a man
on telly with no face and no body was saying:
*'To dump Aron dial 0800 8001. Or, if it's
Michelle you want to dump, add 2, that's 0800
8002 if you want to say goodbye to Michelle.'*
Michelle? Fran paused to confirm she had
been asleep for two episodes. Yep, it was
3.30 pm. She switched off the alarm, then on
and off again, but the noise continued.
There was an emergency siren coming from
outside. She checked online — no updates for
Ash Mountain yet, no need to panic.
'Dad, the town siren's going off,' she yelled
from the hall. 'Not sure why, nothing online. I'm
going to get Vonny, back soon.'
Fran grabbed her backpack and shut the door
behind her.
She knew she couldn't Leave Early, but
expected she'd at least *Believe* Early; and not be
one of those ignoramuses who are like, *Hey take
my pic, Check out Nature, Is that . . . ? Can you
please tell me what I'm seeing?* Believing was
proving difficult, however. To her right, coming

3

in from the north-west, a gigantic wall of black and grey and red, a tsunami of smoke hundreds of metres high, had cut the world in half. She lost a few seconds to disbelief — Was it just clouds? Aliens? The sherry she'd had at 10.20 am? She raced back inside to her bedroom and threw on jeans, jumper, leather boots, gloves, and a beanie. She put a blanket in her backpack, ran down the hall and hugged her dad: 'There's a fire to the north, you follow the drill.' Shutting the front door behind her once more, she checked that all the windows and doors were closed, that the sprinklers were on and the roof damp. She considered the four-wheel drive, but Dante had taken it to the beach with Tiffany. She considered going back inside again and staying there, which would be safe, probably, but she had to be with Vonny, no matter what, so decided against it. She considered the two remaining ostriches and, as per the fantasy she secretly enjoyed sometimes, decided against them.

On foot, the convent hall was a kilometre south-east of the farm. She knew the route too well, every dry inch, and thumbed her phone as she pounced over ditches and dead marsupials.

'Triple Zero,' said a woman. 'What's your emergency?'

'There's a firestorm coming straight for Ash Mountain,' said Fran, breathing in through the nose and out through the mouth. 'It's above McBean's Hill. There are embers — ow, shit. It's coming fast; something's happened. The sky, oh my God, and the wind's gone crazy. No-one knows here, there is nothing online. We need help.' She couldn't hear what the woman was saying — nothing useful. Was she on hold? She hung up and dialled her dad. Engaged.

Somehow, she was still running, and she only winced a little when three kangaroos overtook her, embers landing on their backs from the reddening sky. Thank God, her dad answered this time: 'It's bad, and close,' she said. 'I'm sorry I left you alone there, but I have to be with Vonny. You stick to the plan though. We'll be home soon.'

'On you go,' said Dad.

There was no answer from The Captain, no answer from Vonny. She left voice messages for both as she passed the spreading desert of commuter boxes surrounding the sign:

ASH MOUNTAIN
Population: 867

Feeling the heat as she ran up the walking trail, she dialled home again. 'Dad? I'm seeing flames. Are you okay?'

'All good, it's missing us. Where are you?'

'I'm nearing the monument. Ow, I'm . . . Tell me what to do.'

'Get inside, block both top and bottom doors, and stay in the middle till The Rumbling stops. You'll be fine in there. See you on the other side in fifteen. Go.'

The bluestone tower was on the top of the hill, only twenty metres away, but she was dream-running, not getting anywhere. It was only when she collapsed that she realised the air was no longer air. Like in a panic attack, an asthma attack, she could not squeeze any in. Her eyes were burning and a missile hit her foot. When she felt the pain she scrambled to standing and staggered towards the gothic tower. A eucalyptus bomb hit her back as she opened the thick door. She closed it behind her and looked for rubble to seal the cracks. There wasn't anything suitable — only a used condom, three empty beer cans.

It was so hot, and the world had turned terracotta.

No time to waste on cracks, she ran up the winding inner staircase to close the hatch door at the top. It was already shut. She ran halfway down again, placed herself in the recovery position, and waited for The Rumbling.

★   ★   ★

The sudden still was confusing. She was inside a stone tower, so perhaps that's why there wasn't a breath of a wind, no bird chirping, no town siren. All she could hear was her breathing. It was dusk-dark inside, weak waves of blood-orange light softening the twenty feet above and twenty feet below her curved step. Perhaps it had passed. Perhaps the thick drops of the cool change had brought boys and girls outside into gardens to rejoice in the wet.

It was *too* still. Thunder always accompanied the ecstasy of a cool change.

Maybe she was dead and this was Hades. Growing up she'd often wondered that.

6

Or the wall of grey was a spaceship after all, and she was now inside it. Fran was totally willing to go with the alien hypothesis, but then the silence stopped. A noise. What was that noise?

Several jet engines seemed to be heading towards her.

The Rumbling.

She looked at her watch. 3.37 pm. By 3.52, it should get quiet, and be safe to step outside. She covered her ears and counted sheep, and when they started burning in her mind she counted spoons, and when they melted in her mind she counted . . .

She would count Vonnies, that's what: Veronica.

Beautiful Vonny.

Burning Vonny.

Two minutes in, thirteen to go. She inhaled hot dirt and resolved:

My Vonny.

Fran pulled the beanie over her head, and the blanket from her backpack over her body. She pressed her face to the ground and, for the next thirteen minutes, trembled no more than the seventy-foot rock in which she was encased.

⋆　⋆　⋆

Dear God Dear God Dear God.

Someone was praying, which meant someone was alive. Not Fran, she never prayed, did she? *Dear God, forgive me.*

It *was* Fran. She lifted the beanie from her

7

head, coughed, and covered herself with it again. Holding the blanket over her head, she ascended the stairs on her hands and knees, making one blind plea per step — *Dear God, Please God* — till she reached the top. She wrapped a sleeve round her gloved hand to push the hatch door open, and crawled out onto the edge of the smoking lookout. This was the highest point in the Shire. If Fran took the beanie off, she'd see all the way from the Ryans' to the Gallaghers'. She'd know everything.

Fran did the sign of the cross and said a prayer: 'Forgive me Lord for all the times that I have wished this town burned down.'

She removed the beanie.

2

Ten Days before the Fire

The sign confirmed it. She had arrived in Ash Mountain, the second oldest inland town in Victoria, reputedly. Population, 867. It was 885 when Fran came last; there had been some lucky escapes. One of the Lions must have changed it. When it was her dad's job to repaint the sign, he never did it till the number went up. After the McDonald baby drowned, for example, he waited months; endured a whole lot of pressure from Lion Henry. Luckily, the Ercolini family arrived that winter, aunts and all. Four-year-old Fran had held the paint pot — just over there — while her dad had drawn an optimistic population. The memory was suspiciously smiley.

Vincent sucked her out of it. 'I'll bring Japanese take-away next Friday.'

She wanted to say don't, that it'd be cold by the time they arrived, and that she couldn't imagine eating anything ever again anyway, but instead bit her lip to scare the moan and the crying away; a thing she'd need to do a lot from now on. She'd rather curry if anything at all — it'd travel better — but wasn't about to get all high maintenance with Vincent. They'd coparented the same way they had cohabited, as kind and reliable friends, and should never have flirted with a sexual relationship (they both blamed Tequila, and The Social Club). Whether or not they should have stayed together for sixteen years was another matter. They had a great friendship and a great daughter, who was now sitting in the back of the car. 'Japanese would be perfect,' said easy-going Fran.

Shitboxville, aka the new commuter estate, had totally changed the view. She used to be able to see all the way up to the footy grounds. 'Feels like you two are dropping me at boarding school,' she said, and started to imagine the boys who were dumped here by their families, but then stopped because she hated boarders. She hated this town, and as they turned into the driveway and headed past the ostriches, who were supposed to have died years ago, she imagined there were landmines in the dust-pit encloser. *Boom. Splat. Bird explosions.* She was smiling. She needed therapy. Well, she needed more.

Vonny was still thumbing in the back seat, telling her mate Gayle or Freddie how bollocks her life was, being stuck in this car for the last ninety minutes; and in this shithole for the next two nights.

'When did Gramps get into ostriches?' Vonny asked on behalf of Gayle or Freddie, not looking up.

'When I started getting chased by boys.'

Fran could see herself at fourteen now, running with Olympian determination down the dirt track that was her street, four uniformed boarders close behind and in hot pursuit of a fingering. She was a very fast runner, even then.

10

She reached the house in time and slammed the door, panting. Blazered boys fled round the side and up the hill towards the grandstand and playing fields that backed onto the farm.

'Bloody boarders!' her dad had said, soon after erecting a U-shaped enclosure around the house with three-metre-high electric fences, into which he plonked twelve ostriches. Fran would've rathered a gang-fingering than a prehistoric chastity belt, but her dad did not feel the same, and also had a bit of a thing for ostriches. The birds would stop those boys getting in.

Unfortunately, they would not stop Fran getting out.

There were only two left now — Ronnie Corbett and Mrs Miriam McDonald, although that was not the latter's full title, of course, Gramps often said. 'Being Miriam McDonald of the Drumnadrochit McDonalds, she aye considers herself a cut above the other ostriches, particularly the grimly determined Campbells, and requires to be addressed as Dame Miriam McDonald of Drumnadrochit by everyone, even the Corbetts, who are English, and who she despises and admires in equal measure.'

The birds were almost of an age with Francesca now, and were pointless pets who did nothing but race around horny and shit a liquid stench that Dante had to clean up.

Her belongings, including a desk that had been much used in the city, bumped in the back of Vincent's ute and, as they parked beside her dad's four-wheel drive, she realised she hated this house most of all. She bit her lip again

11

because her dad was waiting inside and she did not hate him, she loved him, which is why she had returned to look after him for the rest of his life.

And hers.

His, just his.

'Hey Mum!' Dante — proof of the failure of the Avian contraceptive device — was waiting on the veranda.

Fran had Dante when she was fifteen, so they never looked right together, not at any stage. Add Vonny and the family unit was even harder to work out.

Vonny had said last visit that the three of them looked like they'd met in the dole queue: 'You've got one underachieving, exhausted, peri-menopausal mother,' ('I am not peri-meno-pausal,' Fran had said) 'one dope-smoking, arty-farty, foody, tattooed, hipster bogan bastard,' (Dante: 'Are you calling me tattooed?') and one pissed-off teenager with different-coloured skin.'

Currently, this perfect teenager was too pissed off to get out of the car.

'Hey baby boy,' Fran said to Dante. Everyone in the family had asked her not to call her twenty-nine-year-old son 'baby boy', but she couldn't help it. That's what he was. A great hugger, too. The best teen mistake she ever made.

A moment later, Dante knocked on the car door. 'It's illegal to leave toddlers in the car,' he said to Vonny. 'Get the fuck out and give your big brother a hug.'

★　★　★

12

She was suddenly in a circle with the rest of her family, everyone silent and staring at Nurse Jen, who was on item number nine now: *The Catheter.*

'Empty the bag before it's three-quarters full. Valves should be used to drain urine at regular intervals throughout the day to prevent urine building up in the bladder.'

Nurse Jen was even less pleasant than the information she imparted, and Fran found herself exchanging naughty looks with Gramps. When she was alone with him, she called him Dad. But otherwise he was Gramps in her mind, had been ever since Dante first said the name. She noticed that a line of mucous had exited Gramps' nose. It was now glistening on his cheek.

'Before and after handling the catheter equipment, wash your hands with warm water and soap,' Nurse Jen said, having obviously decided to ignore the matter on her patient's cheek, despite the fact that almost all her agenda items thus far had related to the wiping of things away.

Fran crossed the circle and sorted her dad with a tissue. 'Grotty bugger,' she whispered. He almost laughed, but he probably wouldn't risk doing that again in public.

Vincent was sitting yoga-perfect, eyes wide and alert. You'd never know he wasn't listening to a word; that he had tuned into an altered state Fran called 'ArseholeLand' once, but never again, after it was pointed out that it was racist. Fran had learned an awful lot since meeting

Vincent, even more since having Vonny, and was always up for confronting her isms. Right now, though, all she wanted to do was confront Vincent's shin with her boot. She was terrified. She needed his help. But Vincent wasn't her partner anymore, which was fine. Fine. It was amazing that he'd driven her here today, that he was bringing Vonny back next weekend. She had no right to expect Vincent's help. Or her grumpy, mother-hating teenage daughter's help. She was alone.

'Any questions?'

Fran had two million, but would rather find the answers herself than spend another minute in the company of Nurse Jen.

★ ★ ★

Dante had made vegan penne for Vonny, and Nonna's lasagne for everyone else, the latter unfortunately reminding Fran of her mother's death, which had ended just like lasagne: all minced flesh and bechamel. She'd been struck by a truck a week before the new highway opened; just seven days before the town was bypassed, trucks and travelling customers rarely seen on North Road again.

The tomatoes were apparently tastier because Dante had tweaked something or other, but she could not taste the difference. The beef came from happy cows, Dante said as he forked some into his gramps' drooped mouth, catching it again when it fell out and giving it to his three-year-old mutt, Garibaldi, who — as usual

14

— was sitting at his feet.

Gramps' eyes were half open, but he was asleep and drooling. His silver head of hair, always so immaculately groomed with comb and Brylcreem, had become thin and scruffy, along with the rest of him.

'Little gems are doing great this year.' Dante was putting the leaves on her plate; damn, she'd never clear it now without hurling or crying or yelling or any combination of the above. She shovelled too much into her dry mouth and wondered if she would ever taste anything ever again.

★ ★ ★

Dante put music on after dinner, a rule he made at the toothless age of six, which is when Fran decided he was old enough to help with the dishes.

'If I gotta wash cups,' wee Dante had said, 'then I do it with 'Candle in the Wind'.'

They had shaken on it. Her boy had come out of her happy and stayed that way. It surprised her, because she had to work at being happy. She often thought she'd never manage without Dante's regular suggestions. For example, Abba, which they sang along to till the place was spotless. Perhaps Dante's father had passed on some positivity and kindness genes. If so, he had kept them well hidden.

It was time to complete the task she dreaded: emptying her belongings into this house. Dante, Vonny and Vincent did most of it. Three trips later and the dining area was filled with suitcases, boxes and one large desk.

Dante was doing a shift at the Old Mill, the only restaurant of the four in the area that did not serve chicken parmigiana. He said three shifts a week was as much of a commitment to anything that he ever wanted to make.

'I'll bring plums tomorrow, we'll make jam,' he said, giving her a hug.

She watched him walk down the driveway, then shut the door behind her. There was crap everywhere. Where to start?

She zig-zagged the huge desk with shoulders and hips till it was under the window. She unpacked and flattened the boxes, leaving one intact and labelling it *Op Shop*. She unplugged the electric can opener on the kitchen bench and put it in the box. Taking its place beside one of the very few power-points on the lino bench would now be her NutriBullet. She switched it on, got a bit of a shock that it worked. She would use it, every day, in this new/old life.

She placed her treasured books on the shelves, realising that each had an inscription:

Happy Birthday Baby Girl, Tiamo! Mama xxx (*The Magic Faraway Tree*)

To My Daughter Francesca on the Occasion of her Birthday, From Dad xxx (*Harry Potter*)

Thought this would look good on your mantlepiece. Ta for the cool name! (Dante's *Inferno*)

Love you, Vincent and Vonny xxx (*Wuthering Heights*, Hardback)

Bless them. All the people she loved — except

Dante — believed in Reading Fran. Fran sometimes believed in Reading Fran too. She probably talked way too much about her and should stop.

She grabbed the suitcases and headed to the northern end of the skinny house. Her teenage bedroom — posters and stickers mostly intact — had been nabbed by Vonny, who was asleep.

Vincent was in Dante's old room, which he had abandoned at the age of sixteen.

'I've found myself,' Dante had said to Fran back then, 'it's Italy I'm looking for now.'

He didn't return for ten years, so his room had been redecorated a couple of times. It was now duck-egg, tranquil, which is probably why Vincent was in it, engrossed on his laptop.

'Night Vin.'

'Night F Face.'

The only room left was the smallest, which froze in winter and boiled in summer. Somehow, Fran had ended up in this container from the age of fifteen, must have had something to do with becoming a mother. One of the walls had been unchanged since the room began life as a studio for the lady of the house; the Florentine floral wallpaper yellowed and peeling, black handprints of various sizes littered over it. Dante had made the first by accident, after Fran sent him out to help paint the door of The Shed of the Dead, one of Gramps' morbid anniversary rituals. Instead of helping, five-year-old Dante had kept trying to open the door, which was forbidden, and then he'd put his hand in the pot of black paint. A small argument, a game of

17

unrequited chasey, a tiny hand print and a large argument had ensued.

Gramps was sick and tired . . . 'Sick and tired.'

They all were. It was a relief when Dante went off to the local state school, and when Fran found a commutable job.

But the three of them missed each other like crazy. The following year, on the anniversary of Sofia's death, Gramps didn't paint the door to The Shed of the Dead. Instead, he dipped his grandson's hand in the pot of sticky black gloss, then pressed it against his beloved wife's Florentine floral wallpaper. Tiny little hands, Dante had.

Till he was twelve, then they expanded werewolf-like all the way to sixteen.

There was a ten-year gap after that, an empty time Fran didn't like to think about, when she wondered if she would ever see him again.

But he came home . . . he came home, and resumed the pawprint ritual with gigantic hands. The wall was fair filling up: Fran would probably need to have a chat with her baby boy soon.

She left her suitcases in the pawprint bedroom and headed back to the living area. The old teak sideboard was still filled with bottles: sambuca, whisky . . . *Ah, there it is*. Sweet sherry. One of the few memories Fran had of her mum was with this very sherry.

She was stirring something on the kitchen bench, smelling it. She had large curly shiny hair that didn't budge no matter what, even when she sneezed, which she always did three times and so loudly that it made Fran jump. She blessed

18

herself as she went along: 'Wah Choo! Bless you.'
She had a small crystal glass, a fairy glass. She
squeaked the cork from the brown bottle and it
clinked when it touched the fairy crystal. When
she took a sip, her face was overcome, bit by bit,
forehead to chin, with happiness.

Five-year-olds weren't allowed to be as happy
as that.

Fran wiped the dust from the bottle, wrenched
off the sticky lid and took a swig.

It wasn't so nice. But she was ready to head to
the other end of the house — the master, with its
en suite; and with her new reason for living.

Her dad was off his head on Oxies, couldn't
move his moving parts, and it took more stamina
than a 10k for her to get his jeans off. She would
never dress him this way again: she could do
something with Velcro, zips maybe. When she
finally fell back, denim in hand, she copped a
devastating first-ever visual of his penis. She and
her dad caught eyes, he saw she saw, and they
both shrugged as if agreeing: *What are you
gonna do?*

Once he fell asleep, she set herself up at the
desk, researching online, and making many lists
of things to do, using different coloured pens
and highlighters and a ruler. She had spent the
afternoon in Office Works, and created a logbook
to keep the various day carers updated. She
laminated important phone numbers and stuck
them on the fridge, including Vincent, her
ex-partner, and Vonny, who was about to become
an even stranger stranger.

By midnight, one wall of the dining-kitchen

was covered in lists, and a workbench had been set up on one half of the desk under the window. She had ordered a great deal of equipment over the last few weeks and, as planned, had just completed her first project, which she would call *Gramps Smokes a Cigarette*. She'd given up trying to get him to quit smoking. What was the point, when he was dying, and when it was the only thing he enjoyed? He didn't enjoy that he couldn't get the fag from his hand to his mouth, though. Two feet off, he was. And he really didn't enjoy someone holding it for him; he said to Fran, 'So close up, and with all the power. No-one's going to dictate the regularity and duration of my drags!' As a potential solution, she'd bought three grabbing implements, one of which — she was pleased to discover — held a Marlboro Light firmly within its claws and had a hinge in the middle. It was just like an arm. She tested it with an unlit cigarette. Perfect. Her dad could manoeuvre this with his hand, and dictate his own drags. Under strict supervision.

She couldn't sleep, and did not understand how anyone could. There was a disabled man in the house. There were horny, geriatric birds in the garden. There were neighbours — nuns, priests, boarders — there were exes and teenage daughters.

Fran bounced out of bed to check on Vonny. For years now, Veronica had been at her best asleep. She removed her girl's earphones and kissed her forehead. But Vonny was not the one who needed to be checked on now. Having just completed twenty-nine years as Mother, Fran

20

would now undertake an indefinite number of years as Carer. Fran peeked through the crack in her dad's bedroom, now cluttered with hospital rails and hoist and wheelchair and bottles and bottles of medications. There was nothing joy-sparking in this room; everything was quite the opposite, but Fran would sort that tomorrow.

She heard nothing, and was relieved.

'Franny?'

Bugger. She took a breath and headed in.

'Sit here.' He had sobered up, and wriggled the fingers on his working hand till she took it in hers.

'You're due an Oxy,' she said.

'Let me make sense for a minute first.'

They looked at his tiny legs at the same time, and it made them both sad.

He always had mountain thighs, her dad — a genetic miracle, as he rarely exercised. 'Hit this!' he used to say to ten-year-old Fran, flexing his muscle, and without hesitation she would punch it really hard. 'You done it yet?' he'd say, no sign of a wince. 'Punch it again.' And Fran would make a better plan and a stronger fist and — *wallop!* — no man could hide the pain from this blow, and yet: 'C'mon hurry up,' he'd say, not even biting his lip.

She could take a really good whack at it now, but having no feeling would take all the fun out of it.

'Can you pass some of that stuff Dante brought over? Works a treat before the pill.' He was pointing at a vegemite jar. Inside were four pre-rolled joints. 'I've decided to spend the rest of my days as a drug addict.'

She knew Dante smoked weed and it didn't bother her; but dealing to his Gramps? Hell, Dante was twenty-nine, had a job, and was happier than she'd ever been; Gramps was seventy-five and practically paraplegic. She let it go, and fetched *Gramps Smokes a Cigarette*, placing the handle in his hand, securing the joint within its claws, and lighting it for him. He manoeuvred it slowly, shaking. Fran had to stop herself intervening several times. She also had to push his head to the side a little so he could take a drag, which he did with gusto.

He seemed to be blowing smoke forever. 'This is not happening to you again, Franny,' he said.

'What?'

He took another drag. 'I'm never leaving this house.'

Fran grabbed the joint and butted it out. 'We've gone over this.'

'I'm never leaving and I'm not letting you stay here, not again. This is not happening to you again.'

She put the Oxy in his mouth and shoved some water his way. She already hated being a carer. People told her it'd make her feel good, but it was making her want to slam her caree's dead leg with a brick. 'What does that mean?'

He nodded at the Oxy bottle, and it dawned on her. 'I'm not leaving your mum,' he said.

Fran had always loved the photo her dad was looking at — her mum riding Millie along the old railway track — and did not like that she was now looking at it angrily.

'This is where I want to die,' he said. 'I'm not asking for your help, just your blessing.'

'Well, fuck off.' So many firsts in one night; she'd never spoken to him like this before. 'You're not getting my blessing. She gathered up his medicine bottles and put them in a pile on the carpet. 'Have you hidden any?'

He shook his head, naughty schoolboy.

Fran lifted the dusty dust-ruffle and crawled under the bed, retrieving the key she had hooked on a spring when she was too old to do that kind of thing. Twenty-seven, she was. For years she had endured a three-and-a-half-hour-plus daily commute from Ash Mountain to St Kilda Road. Each day involved cars, trains, trams and a whole stack of legs. She'd had enough, and was moving to her own weekday flat to achieve the 5:2 life, which was like the diet in that she would be happy some of the time. Dante, eleven, was about to start at the college, despite her protestations that he should stay with her in town, or at least go to any other secondary school.

But he was a country boy, an Ash Mountain boy, and he insisted. He loved living with Gramps: yabbying and shooting boarders with the airgun that Fran had never been allowed to go anywhere near. He and Gramps also enjoyed watching too much television and not doing dishes. And Dante wasn't at all worried about the college. 'It's different now,' he said to his mum. 'Properly co-ed. Anyway I can't be bullied.'

She asked him why not, and he shrugged. 'Just can't.'

He was right. During his four years, no-one

23

dared bug Dayboy Dante; and only one boarder dared add the word Dago to the above nickname, and only once.

Dante still left Ash Mountain as soon as he could, headed off to Rome with a one-way ticket and a medium-sized backpack.

On the day of his flight, Fran made a quiche and a salad and a flask of good coffee. She bought lamingtons and vanilla slices, aka snot blocks, that were nearly as good as the ones from Gallagher's, and put it all in her beloved picnic basket, heading off with the two Vs to meet Gramps and Dante at Tullamarine airport, which Fran had heard a lot about over the years. They would all eat together before seeing Dante off. They'd watch the planes from inside the terminal, take turns to hold Vonny on their shoulders, take the time to get used to all this.

There was nowhere to eat the picnic, no seats with views over runways. Every plastic chair was part of a business, and Fran had thought to bring everything except a lot of money.

She managed to hold it in till Gramps drove off and Vincent started the car. With little Vonny fast asleep in the back, Fran finally cried, tears dropping into the quiche on her lap. No matter what song Vincent found on the radio, her grief intensified to the point that she was convulsing when they turned into Arthurton Road and she accidentally punched the quiche. Window down, she tossed it out, dish and all.

She didn't have to ask Vincent to turn around, and she found most of the quiche. It hadn't shattered like the ceramic.

*   *   *

Fran opened the sliding door of the built-in robe. Before moving to Northcote, she had put her mother's precious, oak linen box in this cupboard, memories safely padlocked inside.

She dragged the chest out onto the bedroom floor and unlocked the padlock as her father watched from his hospital-style bed. She threw the contents into a black rubbish bag. First, the hand-painted birthday cards her mother had given her — one, two, three, four, five birthday cards. In the bin.

'Oi, what are you doing?' Gramps stretched his fingers out.

She ignored him, and took out her mother's precious jewellery box, ballerina intact but out of battery. Inside were two rings: the sapphire and diamond number her dad had proposed with under 'their tree', and a wedding band. She slammed the lid of the pretty box and put it in the rubbish bag.

'Francesca! They're for you.'

'Sorry, I can't hear you because you're dead,' she said, grabbing handfuls of memories now, as much as she could — photo albums and letters and embroidered linen from Italy and her first holy communion dress and the worn koala she'd practically eaten as a toddler. She shoved it all in the black plastic bag.

Wooden chest now empty, Fran put all her father's medications inside and closed the padlock, adding the key to the pile on her keyring and pushing the box into the hall. 'Love you Dad,' she said, turning off the light and half closing the door.

She moved the chest all the way through the living area to the pawprint room. Sliding open the mirrored door of the built-in robe there, she kicked the vacuum cleaner aside and shoved the chest in, putting the black bag of memories behind it and slamming the wardrobe door so hard that it wound up open.

At the desk in the kitchen, she sniffed the joints in the Vegemite jar and texted Dante: 'We need to talk.' She then resurrected the jogging buggy she'd used when Vonny was a baby, and attached a broom to the back, using tie-down straps and masking tape. Then she taped and strapped Vonny's most recently discarded device — a large iPad — to the head of the broom. Her dad's face would be at his actual height (they had argued over this in the past and come to an agreement of five foot eleven). She gave the buggy a wobble. It was a little rickety, but it'd work. Project #2, *Gramps on a Stick*. Tick! He'd leave this house, all right. He'd go to places on a stick he probably wouldn't have gone even before the stroke.

3

Nine Days before the Fire

'Ned Kelly's dad escaped from there,' said her dad, who was not present in the flesh, but speaking from the iPad. He'd been bashful at first, had refused to turn on the video at his end, but obviously couldn't resist. 'Blasted a hole in the old jail the size of an Irishman,' he said. 'They built this tower after that.'

They were at the top of the monument, a place Fran always visited when she was home. She put a coin in the telescope and did a slow 360: there was the city smog, there was the *new* new highway, there was the water tank, there was a digger digging. 'And no-one's escaped since,' she said.

She was ill-balanced when a boarder appeared from behind the bend in the inner staircase of the tower. Her dad's screen banged the bluestone wall, which made him joke-wince, which made Vonny laugh when she shouldn't have because this was one of the things that provoked boarders.

'On you go,' said Boarder #1, flattening himself against the wall and checking out sixteen-year-old Vonny as she slithered past.

There were only three, thankfully. They weren't in uniform, but wearing city-slicker casuals the locals wouldn't be caught dead in.

Even these three were dapper, and they were the dregs of the college, boys who no-one wanted in the summer, bar the clergy.

The boarders remained elevator-silent till they reached the lookout, then one yelled: 'Mountain Slut!'

Fran assumed they'd yelled it to her, then realised that she was now a mountain hag. It was her daughter who was a Mountain Slut. Her head heated as the boys laughed.

'Ignore them,' said Vonny when they were outside. 'Anyway, it's kind of nice to be called a slut for a change. Race you down?' Vonny had inherited her mother's competitive gene, and was off already.

Fran extended the buggy, took hold of the handles, and jogged down the track, her on-screen dad reacting to unexpected potholes with an 'arghhh' and a 'weeee!'.

★ ★ ★

The centre of the thriving metropolis of Ash Mountain was three blocks away. Fran and Vonny headed into Gallagher's Bakery, leaving the window of the four-wheel drive open so her dad could talk to passers-by. He was really getting into the stick thing, and began immediately: 'Boo!'

Henry Gallagher, dressed in his standard shorts/long socks/hat combo, dropped his shopping bag. 'Jesus Christ! Is that you Collins, you bastard? What's your head doing on a pole! Haha!' His wife Shirley had gone nuts apparently, hadn't left the house in years. The shopping was his job.

Since selling the pharmacy five years back, Gramps greeted everyone the same way: 'How's that nasty rash?'

'Itchy,' Henry Gallagher was saying. 'Haha, have you lost weight, mate? No really, how you going?'

Vonny ordered three snot blocks from Tricia, the third Thomas Gallagher girl and the meanest.

'What are you doing for the fete?' Tricia asked.

Fran's blank look encouraged her to explain:

'Australia Day, next Monday on the oval. There'll be games and cakes and rides and stuff. Vonny, you should come.'

Fran always intervened on behalf of her daughter, and was always in trouble for it afterwards. 'You mean Invasion Day?' she said.

Vonny rolled her eyes and tried to make herself smaller, which meant Fran was a bad mother yet again, and that Tricia could add another point to their imaginary scoreboard. Thirty years, and they were still neck and neck.

'It's gonna be respectful and inclusive,' said Tricia.

Fran was surprised she knew the word inclusive. As for respect, what did she ever know about that?

'We've got a competition going among the ethnic minorities in town for the best knitted cat,' Tricia said. 'Vonny, maybe you could try one, y'know, seeing as how you're . . . ' — Tricia whispered the next word as if it was a made up

29

thing — 'indigenous . . . One I made earlier!' she said, pulling a gnarly woollen cat from under the counter. It was life-sized; striped blue, white and red, and scattered with southern stars. Tricia's ethnic minority was obviously 'Australian'.

'Cats are certainly appropriate for Invasion Day,' Fran said, attempting to stand the feral beast on the bench, but its legs were wonky and it fell into the curried egg.

'I'll knit a mixed-up bastard!' Dante had just walked into the bakery and joined the growing line for sandwiches. He kissed his mum, tickled his huffy half-sister, and set about making everyone laugh.

Dante was the best thing about Ash Mountain, and everyone knew it bar Tricia, whose withering look indicated that she did not approve of foul-mouthed bastards with snobby-slut mothers and allegedly aboriginal daughters.

Tricia had a couple of mixed-up bastards of her own from her cousin Chook, so she could stop with that superior look right now.

'I'm not sure mixed-up bastard is a *minority* community here,' said Fran, giving Tricia twenty dollars and herself a point.

'Biggest in town!' said Stephen Oh, who was behind her in the queue. 'Only one that really took hold.'

'Come to think of it, why has there been no chain migration since the Celts?' This was from Verity O'Leary, president of the Country Women's Association and next in the line adjacent, which was for hot food. 'That's how it worked: word of mouth, O'Donaghue to O'Donaghue,

30

Gallagher to Gallagher. Stephen, did you not tell your family and friends about Ash Mountain?'

Stephen reddened because the busy shop had gone silent. 'I told them. But they mostly settled in Leopold. It's . . . it's near, um, the beach.'

Verity and most of the room recoiled, as the in-lander locals did not like to hear mention of the beach. Stephen was fully aware of the error he had made.

'They'll be filling the town pool soon, God willing,' said Verity, who was wanting three curry pies with sauce.

★ ★ ★

'There has been chain migration since the Irish, you know,' said Fran. They'd just passed the Monument Reserve and were now taking in Shitboxville, home to the never-seen commuters.

'Do you know anyone who lives in there?' Gramps hated commuters, they got their prescriptions in Melbourne at lunchtime and their groceries trucked in from Green Creek.

'True, they don't count,' said Fran. 'Guess again.' They drove past the Ash Mountain sign and onto the dirt track. To the left was the dilapidated farmer's cottage that Dante had rented since his glorious return from overseas. There were numerous rusty vehicles and some old furniture in the front yard. Out back was a rickety corrugated iron water tank, which was open at the top and held up by metal stilts.

'Hey, Dad!' Fran waved at their brown brick house to the right. Her real-life dad was with

31

Vincent and Nurse Jen in the living room, his wheelchair facing the thin slice of yellow garden in front of the veranda. Every beaten, grassless foot of the rest of the property was allocated to the two elderly ostriches, still running in order to attract, activities that did not naturally fit together for Fran.

She parked just past the drive to take a look, turning her dad's monitor so he could too. The dominant female, Dame Miriam McDonald, was dashing from one end of the enclosure to the other at about seventy miles an hour. Ronnie Corbett was trying to keep up.

'Day two and he's done in,' said on-screen Gramps.

'Poor Ronnie Corbett.' The light-coloured male ostrich finally stalled and collapsed, and the larger black female pranced off and shrugged with contempt. 'Like getting dumped on *The Love House,* isn't it?'

'Except these birds are wearing more clothing!' said Gramps.

The track was becoming beaten. Just five hundred metres from home and it felt like proper bush, except for the architect-designed two-storey number nestled among the trees: McBean House, owned by Maz and Ciara, who had air-conditioning and a pool and were not afraid to use them. Whenever it was forty plus, it was open house at theirs.

'Hey, why have we gone past our place?' Vonny had only just looked up from her phone.

'Dropping Dad's chainsaw at the Ryans'. Won't be long.'

Vonny slumped in her seat. Everything not on-screen was so annoying. 'Was it the lesbians?' she asked, checking out Maz and Ciara's.

Fran thought they'd abandoned the chain migration convo. 'Unfortunately, no,' she said. Ash Mountain was unnerved by the kind of joy Maz and Ciara shoved in their faces — theatre trips and open houses! — which is why there'd been a for-sale sign in their garden for eighteen months. 'Nup,' she said, 'this chain migration started in 1901, which is when . . . '

'Federation,' Vonny, messaging her friends at the same time, said. 'History-lesson time: gonna kill my mother.'

'Yeah, but that's not it.' Fran always used to get a little carsick on this track. She opened the window in case. 'In 1901 the brothers came to Ash Mountain.' This was a new theory for Fran, but she thought it a goody — that before the internet, the colleges were like niche sites on the deep web, bringing people together from every which way, a community of individuals with one thing in common: boys age eleven to sixteen. 'And that caused the one chain migration that has thrived since the Irish.' She reached the end of the tree-lined driveway and parked by the bean garden. 'Perverts,' she said, popping the boot and turning to Vonny. 'So just take it in for me, hey?'

'What? Me? No way. In there?'

The Victorian weatherboard farmhouse was in need of a paint, and the wrap-round veranda could do with some repair, but it was still the prettiest place Fran had ever seen. 'Knock on the door, give it to whoever answers, and we're outta here.'

'What if a sexual pervert answers?'

'Jeez, okay, we'll both go in. And out. In and out.' She switched off the engine and said to Gramps: 'Won't be long,' but he'd turned his video off, probably when she started talking about the brothers. She took a breath and got out of the car. It was time to face Brian Ryan Junior again.

4

Thirty Years before the Fire

The last time Fran spoke to Brian Ryan Junior
she was fifteen, around Vonny's age, and walking
back from town along Ryan's Lane. The Blue
Light Disco was on that night, and Fran was
thinking about how great she was going to look
in her new acid-wash jeans, when his father,
Brian Ryan Senior, appeared on the track about
a hundred metres ahead.

'Fran! Fran Collins, stand in the middle of the
road, there. Stop! Do not move!' He rustled
people as he did his sheep, retching orders in
guttural shards. 'FRAAAAAN!'

She would always obey Brian Ryan Senior,
who, after all, may have been asking her to freeze
in order to save her life. There was obviously a
nearby snake, bull, plague of locusts, truck,
bogan, kangaroo, boarder, priest, brother, nun,
spider, ostrich, magpie . . .

'Stand there Fran, good — I'm letting some
sheep out of this paddock.'

She began breathing again, phew.

'They'll run towards you but if you don't
move they'll stop. Okay? Just don't move and
they will stop.'

Fran did not have time to consent before at
least fifty sheep poured out onto the road ahead.
One looked her way, causing several to turn and

check her out too, because she was standing still like that, in the middle of the road.

She understood why they charged.

'Don't move! Fran, do not move,' Brian Ryan Senior said.

At least two hundred sheep there were, but they were attacking as one, with so many eyes and so many hoofs that were swirling and merging and thundering at her, no way were they going to stop.

She did a netball dodge and scaled a tree.

'Stupid idiot girl!' Brian Ryan Senior said, setting off after his scattering flock — for several days, rumour had it.

His geeky seventeen-year-old son, Brian Ryan Junior, skulked after him, stopping at the foot of Fran's tree as if by accident and not looking up to say: 'You need a hand down?'

'No,' said Fran, and when he started walking off, she added 'Weirdo'.

★ ★ ★

Fran had spotted the acid-wash jeans in the window of the London Emporium two weeks prior to the Blue Light Disco. Ash Mountain's answer to a department store was located beside Gallagher's Bakery on North Road. It was a double-fronted weatherboard cottage with quaint verandas and a creaky door that it took a lot of courage to open. Three times in the last fortnight Fran had chickened out — first, a group of boarders were walking by; next time she spotted Tricia Gallagher inside; time after that, someone

36

had put flowers on The Spot where her mum died and she had to go home and cry. The street was clear of aggressors and grief now, and Tricia was in hospital due to a sheep-dipping incident. Safe, she went in.

This would be her debutante disco. For many hours she had imagined herself arriving at the dance wearing the acid-wash jeans — *Wow, you look amazing,* everyone would be saying, *Check your figure, girl!* — and her chest was spasming as the shop's door creaked closed behind her. Mrs Beatrice Gallagher, reading a magazine at the counter, hadn't approved of Fran since she won Best and Fairest at netball (Tricia, her most talented daughter, won Most Improved). She had fifties, curly dark hair and cats-eye glasses, which she looked over to accuse her only customer thus: 'Can I help you?'

'Just looking,' Fran said, too nervous to approach the subject of the jeans in the glass enclosure. She knew she would need the assistance of the mother of her frenemy in order to pull this off, but was still unsure how best to get it. Her father had given her a fifty-dollar note the night before, and it was wet in her palm. She had planned it all out. She was going to buy the acid-wash jeans, and the Olivia Newton John off-the-shoulders lavender top she had spied on the sales rack from the window. She would also require a new pair of shoes to set the whole thing off, as her own collection consisted of one pair of thongs, two pairs of runners, one pair of Blunnie boots, and one pair of black school shoes.

There was one of everything in the London

Emporium — one wedding dress, one debutante dress, one blue tie, one 34B bra, one pair of acid-wash jeans, one lavender off-the-shoulders Olivia Newton John top. Fran had prayed the previous night that the jeans would be a size ten because she suspected that something had happened around her thigh area recently. Having examined the tag from outside, she knew the jeans were the same cool brand Erin Donoghue wore to Margherita Delia's sixteenth, but she did not know the price, or the size. Please be ten, please be ten. She was heading towards the cabinet. Soon, she would ask Mrs Gallagher if she could try them on, please.

'Trying 'em on or what?' Mrs Gallagher was behind her, with keys.

'Not sure.' Fran tried her best to be nonchalant, which made Mrs Gallagher huff and about-face. Fran found herself shrieking, which was not in the plan at all: 'Okay, I'll try them on, yeah, that'd be great.'

The opening of the glass cabinet was a solemn ceremony, which Mrs Gallagher undertook with great slowness. Fran was hyperventilating with anticipation when the ritual ended and the jeans were handed over. There was only one changing room, directly beside Mrs Gallagher's counter, and the curtains did not meet. Fran took off her shoes and began to pull the jeans up under her dress, catching the old bag perving twice before realising the sad truth. The acid-wash jeans would not pass her thighs. She twisted her back while reading the label: size eight, bugger. $49.99. Damn. 'Ow.'

'Need a hand?'

Oh Lord, this was not the voice of the mother, but of Tricia Gallagher herself, who was supposed to be in hospital. 'Oh, hi, Tricia. No, no, all good.' It wasn't, though. Fran's back-twisting injury was the kind that makes breathing hurt, so she decided to do that very little. There was no way to get the jeans on, and it was proving very difficult to get them off, particularly while not breathing.

'You're not size eight, are ya?'

Tricia's words made her inhale, probably a good thing. Screw teeny-tiny Tricia Gallagher, whose sheep-dipping injury had obviously been way exaggerated, no sling or bandage or nothing.

Despite a curtain-opening malfunction, Fran exited the changing room with attitude and jeans: 'They're perfect, ta, I'll take them.'

They did not fit her. They had cost all her money. She had been unable to offset the outfit with the lavender off-the-shoulders Olivia Newton John top, even though it was on sale, and did not have a pair of suitable shoes. At the end of the small strip of shops, Fran began running. She would run all day every day between now and the Blue Light Disco. She would eat nothing but watermelon. She held off till the monument carpark, then cried while running all the way home, her terrible jeans swinging in her London Emporium bag.

5

Nine Days before the Fire

Her dad had offered Brian Ryan Junior a lift home after that fateful Blue Light Disco, and just before arriving at this beautiful farmhouse, Fran had vomited in the back seat. Her zipper had burst at some point during the evening and blackberry nip bile was dripping all the way down her stomach. Her feet were bleeding, she had lost her dead mother's shoes, and she did not want to be in a car with Brian Ryan Junior, nor look him in the eye ever again.

The week after the disco, Brian Ryan Junior ran away from home to be a vegetarian, reappearing twenty-eight years later as a sad vegan with four children and a new name: The Captain.

Seriously.

Weirdo.

She felt like vomiting now too. She should stop thinking about acid-wash jeans and just knock on the door. Thankfully, Vonny did it for her.

Twin girls, around nine, answered, both wearing nothing but a large T-shirt.

'Have you got any cheese?' asked one.

'Amy!' said the other, before correcting: 'You got any cheese, *please?*'

A thirteen-year-old-ish girl, dressed in jeans

40

and a short T-shirt, intervened, slapping the one who wasn't Amy on the back very hard: 'Scat! Sorry about them. Oi! Get off that! AMY!' The girl disappeared to get Amy off something, and was immediately replaced by a sixteen-year-old girl. Fran wondered if girls might continue to appear this way all the way to ninety, and was beginning to understand their father's new nickname. She wouldn't be surprised if she soon heard a whistle.

'Can I help you?' This teenager had the apron, hair and joylessness of a Victorian farmer's wife.

'I'm Fran Collins, from next door, and this is my daughter, Veronica — Vonny.'

Vonny said 'hi' as politely as she could, which was rudely. It was a relief that this girl —

'Rosie,' she said, no smile.

— was even ruder.

'Dad asked me to drop this off, so I'll just pop it here, shall I?' Fran was about to put the chainsaw on the ground and get the hell out of there when:

'Fran! Fran Collins!'

Guttural shards had turned out to be hereditary.

'It *is* you!'

A middle-aged man was standing in front of her. If she looked hard, she could see that his teeth were the same, but nothing else. He had been stretched and redrawn and it had turned out well.

'Congratulations on keeping your hair,' she found herself saying. Brian Ryan Junior had turned out to be a silver fox. He hugged her as if they were old friends, and she forgot the Blue Light Disco for a moment.

'I've made fudge,' he said. 'Come.'

They had no choice, so followed him into his vegan tree-changer's kitchen. The fudge smelt good. The twins had been put in charge of icing it.

'Rosie, take Vonny and get a handful of mint, yeah?' said Brian Ryan Junior.

Both girls looked horrified, which somehow spurred both adults to make this happen, no matter what.

'Can I have your phone before you go, V, need to check something.' Fran extended her hand, and Vonny met it slowly and with hatred. There was a slight tug of war, which Fran won, and the girls headed off to bond over herbs.

'I wanted to talk to you about something,' said Brian Ryan Junior, shooing away his icing-covered twins and cutting a piece of fudge for Fran.

That fudge! Perhaps Brian Ryan Junior would be The Captain to her from now on . . . The Captain.

'I took a wedding booking for next Monday, from Emily Nelson.' He was showing her a photo of a woman on his laptop. Blonde extensions and Botox, a Real Housewife of Melbourne type.

Fran didn't understand what he was talking about, and needed another piece of fudge. 'Your little girls really seem to want some cheese,' she said, keen to stick to food-related conversations.

He sighed. 'I know.'

'I can get them some, if you like, it'd have

42

nothing to do with you.'

He thought for a moment then shook his head. 'I'd never agree to that.'

Fran shook her head and helped herself to another piece of fudge. 'No, well of course you wouldn't.'

They smiled, the deal was done.

He was showing her something, the woman on his laptop, that's right. 'I don't get eyebrows these days,' she said. This Emily woman's were jet black and over-arched. 'So she's getting hitched in your shearing shed?'

'Next Monday.'

'And you're telling me because . . . ?'

'Because she's marrying this man.' The Captain zoomed out to include the man on Emily's arm.

Fran was now looking at The Boarder. Thirty years on and he was exactly the same, but this was not a good thing. His hair should have greyed. His shoulders should have rounded. His smile should have altered. Blackberry nip — she could taste it, and it was rising. She put her hand over her mouth.

The girls were back with the mint and it was clear neither were happy.

'You going to the dance?' The Captain said to Vonny, who was wanting her phone back, and to shoot Fran in the head.

'The Blue Light Disco, in two hours, Rosie's going. You could go together.'

'So sorry,' said Vonny, 'I've got nothing to wear.' She now looked like she wanted to shoot everyone in the head, with a machine gun.

'Rosie has so many clothes!' said The Captain. 'Stay. You girls should get ready together. What do they call it? 'Prees'? Pre-drinks. Non-alcoholic, obvs.' He stared out his daughter, who was still wearing the apron and a very unhappy expression.

Rosie had blinked before her dad, and was therefore required to play host to Vonny. 'You wanna?'

'Okay, cool,' Vonny said, putting her hand out to retrieve the phone from her mother, then following her new friend to the bedroom.

'Blue Light Disco?' Fran said to The Captain.

And this is what The Captain said to Fran: 'They're much safer these days.'

6

Thirty Years before the Fire

Her dad had done his best, but she could really do with a mum right now; a living one with bigger feet. After the London Emporium fiasco, he had been so upset for his little girl that he had entered The Shed of the Dead for the first time in ten years, which is when he'd packed his wife's every belonging into boxes and locked the double doors. The shoes shocked Fran. High heels with sexy Italian names, like Amalfi by Rangoni and Silvia Fiorentina. Fran couldn't imagine wearing anything like this, or being closely related to a dead woman who had. She had slept with one particular photo album from the age of five to ten, and realised she should not be surprised by the shoes. Her mother, Sofia Biagi, was North Carlton's answer to Sofia Loren. She was a woman with curves, and had worn outfits to accentuate them.

Fran had obviously inherited her father's practical fashion genes. But not tonight. Tonight she was all over Sofia Loren. She hadn't been to an event like this before, one with boys and music and no parents. It had been more than a year since the attempted gang-fingering episode and the arrival of the ostriches, and it had taken a lot of apricot bottling to persuade her dad to let her go — she still had calluses on her hands from pipping those things. Having made the decision, they were both determined to make this the happiest night of Fran's life.

They decided on a pair of silver glitter shoes with a three-inch heel because they had an open toe, which might allow her extra size and a half to spill out. The jeans required a wire coat hanger and a lot of lunging from one corner of the bedroom to the other. She was moving a tad like Dame Miriam McDonald, in fact. Maybe that bird was just wanting to get into her jeans too. The top had been more difficult to sort, until her dad had a brainwave, taking a pair of scissors to the shoulders of a shrunken black t-shirt and announcing: 'Oliva Newton Who?'

She did look perfection — you could hardly see the zip strain at the very top of the jeans, not if she kept the scissored T-shirt in place, which would mean no arm-dancing, which would be fine, as Fran had never danced in public with her legs, let alone her arms. The only time all limbs had been on fire, along with everything else in her body and brain and soul, was in her bedroom with 'Wuthering Heights'. *It's me, I'm Cathy . . .* Freedom so dangerous it only existed behind a locked door. Kate herself had probably only pulled it off in that field cos there was security.

Earlier, Fran's dad had presented her with a bucket of reduced-price makeup from his chemist. He'd never let her wear makeup before, let alone brought her these colourful beauties in their clicking plastic cases. She organised them on her chest of drawers, by facial area, and then by colour. She opened and shut them, smelt and touched them: mascara, nail polish, dark-brown foundation. She was having a ball, and ended up deciding on green eyeshadow, liquid eyeliner, pink rouge and bright-red lipstick. Once she was certain she was truly perfection, she cat-walked into the lounge with aplomb: *ta-da*.

Her dad pounced from his brown velour, moving-parts armchair. 'By Jove, I think she's got it!' He then turned up the volume on his record player, waltzing a solo celebration to The Seeker's 'The Carnival Is Over'.

'Honestly, Dad, that song?' She kissed him goodnight. 'At the beginning!'

Heels in plastic bag, runners on feet, Fran took off down the driveway, waving back to her twirling, melancholic father before powering towards her town of Ash Mountain.

7

The Day of the Fire

GRAMPS

There she went, running down that track again.

'*To dump Aron dial 0800 8001,*' someone on the telly was saying. '*Or, if it's Michelle you want to dump, add 2, that's 0800 8002 if you want to say goodbye to Michelle. Who goes? You decide.*'

It was a difficult one. Michelle was cruel and wore bikinis. Aron was kind and did not bring anything to the party.

The Drill was that he should do two things when asked to follow it: he should dial Triple Zero, and he should park his wheelchair in the middle of the hall because help would arrive. *Help would arrive.*

He was never much of a rebel, only and often rebel-adjacent, but was already failing to follow The Drill. He was in his bedroom, looking out at the dust pit he had imprisoned himself in till the end of the world, which was now, apparently — it was even the end for this house, the safest in the Shire, nothing but brick and dirt.

He was supposed to follow The Drill.

'Hello Google,' he said.

Fran had installed the device the day after she

arrived, along with many of her other suicide-prevention solutions, and had made him practise for over an hour.

The machine was not responding. Oh, he remembered, he had to say hillo for hello and Boogie instead of Google. 'Hillo Boogie,' he said.

'*Hillo*,' replied Boogle.

Outside was the hell he imagined he'd go to if he swallowed the pills. Armageddon was visibly and rapidly heading this way. The heat from the window panes hurt the parts of him that still felt, and he was surprised not to revel in it. For months he had prayed to feel anything, this . . . yes, give me agony, and yet he found himself pressing a button and moving away from the heat of the glass, away from the main attraction, the flames that were now visible outside, saying, *Ha ha, I know, right? I told ya over and over, yet you were still, 'She'll be right.'*

'What is it like to burn to death?' Gramps said to Boogie.

It sounded bad, and Gramps found himself thinking of his medication, which was in the small bedroom, in a chest, locked.

'Stop. Call Vonny,' he said to Boogie, and was astounded when it worked. 'Vonny, are you okay? Where? Vonny . . . ' He was cut off, and Fran was calling. She should hide in the monument, he said, praise the Lord he had something to say to his baby girl. 'See you on the other side in fifteen. Go.'

Boogle went dead, along with the lights and the telly.

He was stoned. While his daughter was

napping in the lounge, he had managed to retrieve the vegemite jar and attach a joint to the claw of the reacher grabber.

That's right, the world was on fire. The windows were rumbling. Tornadoes were flying into the enclosure. Miriam and Ronnie were going bananas.

His wife's ashes were in a pale-blue biscotti tin on the bookshelf in the hall. He parked his chair beside it and with his finger coaxed the tin until it balanced precariously between the shelf and his limpy knee. One wrong move and Sofia would wind up on the gold carpet. He made three carefully considered moves, each involving a finger wriggle and/or chair acceleration. He'd done it. Sofia would be with him.

He made his way to the kitchen bench and removed the landline's handset with his teeth, dropping it onto the tin in his lap. Having manoeuvred the chair to the correct angle, he was now able to complete part one of The Drill, by pressing the buttons on this mustard relic with his nose.

From the kitchen bench he could see out onto the enclosure. Miriam was running harder and faster than she ever did when enticing Ronnie, which no-one would think possible.

There was no fire in here, no flames near the phone, and yet the skin on his hand was changing.

Gramps was impressed with the accuracy and speed of his nose-dialling.

Outside he saw that Ronnie Corbett's wing was smoking.

He left the handset dangling from the counter and headed for the hall, where — according to The Drill — he should park himself until help arrived.

'Thank you for your call,' an automated voice was saying.

But he was not parking his chair in the hall, he was heading for the door. He was using his teeth to open it.

Where was *Gramps Opens a Door* when he needed it, *Gramps Puts Out a Fire*, *Gramps Saves His Family*? If he ever got this door open, it would be an agonisingly slow journey down the ramp to the ostrich gate, and so far he was unable to grip the smouldering lock with his teeth. He'd heard somewhere that most people are heroes in disaster situations, but that probably didn't include people who could only open things with their teeth.

He sacrificed his lips to grip the lock, and opened the door. As he left the house that he had built for his family, he heard a woman's voice. It was coming from the dangling handset in the kitchen: 'Thank you for your call,' the voice repeated.

And before the door slammed and the telephone lines toppled, he heard the rest: 'You have voted to say goodbye to Aron.'

8

Thirty Years before the Fire

Fran stopped at the monument to replace her runners with the open-toe heels. She had a hand mirror in her bum bag, and looked herself over before dumping her shoes at the top of the tower and heading down the track. Blisters were well on their way by the time she stopped at the ten-foot-high, full-body statue of Bert Gallagher, erected to much furore, as he had killed himself due to losing all his money at the races. The debate regarding the statue's erection had allegedly become more heated than the one involving the renaming of Massacre Gully.

At the oval, she sat at Bert Gallagher's feet and downed the blackberry nip she'd poured into her bottle. She gagged twice, just managing to keep it down, then stood up as a confident Sofia Loren, who she would remain until she reached the double doors of the convent hall. She had friends waiting inside — of course she had friends — so there was no fear in pushing open the doors. Tricia, one of these friends, would be waiting for her in the foyer, as agreed. At the time, she didn't realise how sad this was, that she hated her friend more than anyone in the world, and that her friend hated her even more, enough to say when she opened the door:

'Told ya you'd need a ten! The zip's bursting!'

Tricia was finding this so funny. 'I can see your undies!'

Sofia would probably have had something excellent to say back, but Fran was Fran again, her zipper wide open, she realised, her strawberry-themed briefs on show.

Tricia and her two new friends — Tricia was really popular all of a sudden — continued to giggle as Fran gathered herself and made her way across the empty dance floor, wobbling in her heels at first, every bit forty-nine-dollars and ninety-nine cents. The dance floor was large and empty, yet another song of the unhappily privileged adding to the depressed vibe. 'Down in Kokomo', this one. She'd love the DJ to play Cher or Kylie, or something indicative of the empowerment of the times. Nowadays girls could be sexy if they wanted to be, like Fran was now in her acid-wash jeans, and they could be glamorous and angry too, if they wanted to be. The girls' convent school, attached to this hall, had just closed forever. Thank God for that. The brothers' college was cleaning up its act and taking in fifth and sixth-year girls after the summer. Fran was going to be one of twenty girls to go there, and the music was making her excited about it. Blue and red and white dots pinged all round, and by the time she reached the middle the DJ put on 'Handle Me with Care', a song she didn't know well or particularly like, but it caused her to stop suddenly and fling off her heels, right there below the disco ball, the floor all hers to shapeshift the dots of light.

It's me, I'm Cathy!

It was a good while later when she opened her eyes to find Brian Ryan Junior doing the white man's overbite. 'Sorry about the sheep.' He leaned in to say this; must have just had a mint; would have totally ruined her mood if she hadn't noticed the cute boarder in the corner. He was liking what he was seeing and she was liking being it.

It was *The Boarder*, as it turned out, but Fran didn't know that then.

9

Nine Days before the Fire

Fran realised she was driving home from The Captain's at ten km an hour, and that she was afraid. The Boarder was coming to Ash Mountain. She hadn't seen him for nearly thirty years. She had hoped to not see him for another thirty.

Nurse Jen's car was still in the driveway, but Vincent's ute was gone. She checked her phone — and Vincent had texted:

Heading off F Face — your dad seems settled w the nurse. Remind V to confirm her bus time tomorrow. See you Friday and ring any time, here for you xx

Fran drove on fifty metres and turned right into Dante's. She knew she shouldn't rely on her son's friendship so much, but she did. He was the only person she felt no shame with. 'The Boarder's getting married up the road next Monday,' she said as soon as he opened the door.

His apron was covered in tomato. 'I'll settle the *sugo*,' he said, 'you pour the wine.'

A minute or two later they were in the back garden, although 'garden' might have been too strong a word. The half-acre was filled with her son's enthusiasm for new projects and his lack of interest in old ones. 'I'm an ideas man,' he said if

55

ever asked. 'I'm not supposed to follow things through.' This year was all about lettuces, pottery, chooks, and tomatoes. He was also drawing up plans to turn the rusty old water tank into a treehouse; part of a long-term mission to make his property an artist's retreat and outdoor gallery.

Fran lit one of the cigarettes she'd hidden in Dante's shed.

'Why would he be doing it here, in Ryan's Lane?' he said.

'He might want to see his bastard son, show off or something, make amends, the prodigal father.'

'Or he might want to see his slutty ex-girlfriend,' Dante said.

'I was never his girlfriend.' She was slutty though. 'Hey, guess where Vonny's going tonight — the Blue Light Disco.'

'She's unlikely to get knocked up, at least.'

'She's going with Rosie Ryan.'

'Is Rosie gay?'

'Dunno. Be great if Von's got a weekend pal here. So, do you want to see your long-lost father or what?'

'No.'

'We could hide behind a tree and watch them come out of the church.'

'Not a good plan. He won't have given us a second thought; honestly, Mum, there's nothing to see and nothing to worry about. I'll stay out of his way, but if I bump into him I'll stay calm.'

'I won't manage that.'

'No,' said Dante. 'You should stay well away.

You should go to Bali.'

'I'm never going to go to Bali.' She'd never go anywhere ever again.

'Shut up, yes you will.'

'Is it seven already? Promised I'd take Gramps to mass. By the way, no more dealing to your grandfather.' Fran butted her fag and headed inside to the bathroom, where she had her own toothbrush. 'The Boarder probably assumes there's no way I'd still be in this dump,' she said.

'I like this dump,' said Dante.

Fran spat out toothpaste, wiped her mouth, and kissed her son's forehead. 'Yeah, but you're a dickhead.'

10

Nine Days before the Fire

DANTE

Vonny was getting altogether too cool to talk to her big brother every day. He'd tried several times and she wasn't answering. He stirred the Bolognese and messaged her: *Guess who's getting married in town next Monday?*

No time 4 this, Vonny typed.

The Boarder

He still hadn't piqued her interest. *As in THE Boarder, my biological father*

Holy shit

Still not important enough for her to call.

Will you come have a squiz with me at the church? I just want a look?

Course

Don't tell Mum.

They must have said this to each other a million times over the years.

Obv!! Xx, Vonny replied.

Dante was cooking for the girl whose dating profile was on his screen. Tattooed Tiffany who 'eats anything'.

He tasted the Bolognese — it was not special enough for Tiffany. He cooled some on a saucer and gave it to Garibaldi, who seemed to agree.

58

Dante went outside and picked some rosemary, basil and a sprig of thyme. He checked there was water and seed in his bird stand. His faithful dog followed him to the chicken hutch, where ten happy chooks lived the good life.

Howie in particular looked very healthy, Dante thought, picking him up. 'Hey Howie!' He then placed the chook on the chopping block and, axe in hand, swung once and severed Howie's head.

Vonny had become a vegan when she saw him do this. She told him she still had nightmares that there was a ginormous headless chicken running round and round her house.

Dante waited till Howie slowed, then carried him and his head inside.

Cacciatore, he was thinking.

11

Nine Days before the Fire

Gramps was grumpy when Fran got home and no longer wanted to go to mass. 'I've decided to take up Satanism,' he said. ''Do what thou wilt'.'

Fran and Nurse Jen agreed he would probably change his mind. He'd never missed mass. Even when he was in hospital he had Father Frank do home deliveries. Nurse Jen agreed to stay on till 8.30, and Fran ended up in the second back row of St Michael's with Gramps on a Stick beside her in the aisle. He hadn't turned his iPad on yet. He would.

Fran always went to mass when she visited her dad, and always hated it. Nothing had changed in thirty years. If she could, she went to the Saturday 7.30 pm mass, because it was the fun one, in relative terms. Sunday 8.30 had its good side — it was fast, forty minutes at most — but this was outweighed by the ungodly hour and The Mons's grim reaper sermon, which always led to seven days of depression. Rumour had it The Mons had been sent to the parish in the eighties to 'keep an eye', but the official story was that he had family in the area. Sunday 10.30 mass was the big show, run by Father Alfonzo in Fran's childhood and adolescence, and by Father Frank after Father Alfonzo was arrested. You had to wear something decent to the 10.30.

It was always either boiling or freezing and always went on for at least ninety minutes.

As ever, it was standing room only at the Saturday 7.30. The seats were mostly taken by farmers and their young ones, many of whom would be dipping sheep in the morning. Teenagers whispered and giggled at the back, some of the girls wearing a conspicuous disposable layer, no doubt on top of their *ta-da* outfits. They'd have somewhere to go afterwards, like the Blue Light Disco, and according to Verity O'Leary there was a pancake night on at the church hall to raise money for the proposed new statue. 'Many of us feel,' Verity said as she took a pew, 'that Bert should be replaced by something — and someone — *sturdier*.'

Halfway through a letter from St Paul to the Corinthians, Gramps' voice bellowed from his screen: 'Did you bring ten dollars for the collection?'

Sister Mary Margaret, five rows down, gave Fran a dirty look.

Pervy old witch.

'Yep,' Fran said, turning down the monitor's volume and joining a synchronised sitting-down. It was time to watch people line up to eat the actual no-kidding flesh of the saviour.

'Body of Christ,' said Tricia Gallagher's twenty-six-year-old daughter, whose skirt had been tucked into the bottom of her undies all the way from the tenth row up to Father Frank. Someone should have told her. Maybe Fran should have told her. Ash Mountain wasn't a kind place.

'Body of Christ,' said Mrs Ercolini, hands cupped to receive her Jesus-meat.

Oh dear — Sister Mary Margaret had taken to the stage and was conducting a choir of very poor singers. In the past, this was the only part Fran enjoyed, but they were singing a modern, happy-clappy number and it was impossible to join in.

It was only 8.05. If her dad switched his monitor off again, she'd sneak out. If he didn't, perhaps she could manufacture a malfunction and sneak out anyway.

And stand. And Our Father who aren't in heaven, Holy Spirit, Amen, Sit, Stand, Sermon.

Father Frank always enjoyed his moment on stage, and so did all the footy fans in the congregation, which was almost everyone. Every week he relayed a special moment from The Bombers' latest game, as if it was going to be a metaphor for something, but it never was. Father Frank just liked talking about the footy.

The end was in sight: it was time for the 'peace be with you'. Fran turned to shake the hand of the person she'd been sitting next to, realising it was The Captain's thirteen-year-old daughter. What was her name again?

'Peace be with you, Mrs Collins,' she said.

'Please call me Fran — I've forgotten your name!'

'It's Cathy.'

'Peace be with you, Cathy. Where's your dad?'

'He's not into God.'

She liked that The Captain wasn't into God. 'You need a lift home?'

'Mrs O'Leary's taking me after pancakes, but thanks.'

The collection plate had arrived. Fran didn't have the ten dollars her dad insisted on donating each time; she had two. She put one in and passed the plate to the woman sitting behind her, careful not to make eye contact in case she knew her too.

★   ★   ★

Mass had made her nauseous — Father Frank and Sister Mary Margaret always turned her stomach. Back at the house, she saw Nurse Jen off, surprised at how quickly she'd changed her opinion of the woman; an officious old bag was exactly what she needed right now.

Fran found herself kissing her sleeping dad's forehead the way she did with Vonny and Dante. He was her baby now, too. She walked back along the thin hallway, one end of which was lined with bookcases, and wriggled her fingers at the Biscotti tin on the middle shelf. After her mum died, and if no-one was within earshot, she always said 'Hey Mum, love you', when she walked past the ashes, which were to remain on the middle shelf until her dad was also in the tin. Eventually, the ritual softened to a finger wave, the mantra said inside her head.

She poured herself a sherry and sat at the kitchen bench. In three decades, the house had changed about as much as mass. The same books were on the same shelves, including classics like *War and Peace* and *Pride and Prejudice*, and one entire bookcase was dedicated to the *Encyclopaedia Britannica*, which her dad still preferred over Google. For as long as Fran could remember, every question she asked her dad ended with the same response. For example, age eleven: 'What does 'rags' mean? Tricia said Melissa smells cos she got her rags.'

'Get me M, Franny,' he'd said, taking up position at the end of the dining table as she reached for the gigantic, burgundy-leather, gold-embossed volume. He searched for the correct page while she made him a fresh cup of tea, excited to discover the meaning of rags, which had something to do with the letter M.

The tea had to be just right: 'Heat the pot, the steel one next to the toaster, not the ceramic one on the shelf, which pours poorly and should be taken to the Op Shop or thrown out. Heat the cup, cup not mug, put half an inch of cold milk in the cup — full cream, not half, not skim; cold, not hot, not warm — and half fill the pot — half — with freshly boiled water. Two bags of Tetley's best in for two minutes, Franny, one hundred and twenty seconds before the slow pour. Do not meddle, do not rush — perhaps use a timer — do not wriggle, and for God's sake do not squeeze.'

Apparently, her mum was crap at tea, didn't take it seriously at all. Coffee, well that was another matter. Fran was torn. She'd probably choose tea anytime after lunch, or if she needed to diffuse an awkward moment — like if someone had just died. However, first thing every morning she needed coffee the way her mum did, downing it warm and in one like the drug that it is.

Fran worked best with clear directions, and her dad was always appreciative. She had made the perfect brew while he prepared to read all about menstruation, glasses hanging off the end of his patrician nose. He turned to the correct page with freshly scrubbed fingers that lapped the thin paper, air wafting towards his thin nostrils. The *Encyclopaedia Britannica* smelt glorious, even when it was about to inform you all about fanny blood. Information was a luxury back then. Probably why Fran never had much.

Now, sitting with her sherry, she stared at Gramps' favourite mismatched set of crockery, which was on the dining table, ready for the strict three-course breakfast he was hoping to make himself six months ago and would never get to make again. The house smelt of toast crumbs. Even if she cleaned the toaster, tray included, and the rest of the kitchen, it still smelt of toast crumbs. Once fresh and pleasant things, they were very disagreeable when stale and stuck inside a low-ceilinged seventies box, its windows suffocated by dense fly-wire screens. You could either have air, or no flies, and Gramps had chosen the latter.

There was another smell too, perhaps the small compost bin by the sink that no-one had fed to the garden since the stroke. Or the dirty water in the bucket under the shower, with indescribable floaties on top. Fran got up and emptied both onto the shrubs in the thin strip of back garden, most of which had already failed to survive the summer.

The house was dirty. Maybe it always had been. Back at the kitchen bench, Fran wrote on the back of an unopened Simply Energy bill: *DEEP CLEAN HOUSE,* adding a moment later, *PAY ELECTRICITY BILL.* She closed her eyes and took a moment to be mindful. It was so quiet. She was so alone.

She was failing to be mindful, her lip was trembling.

Boom!

The noise couldn't have been the ostriches — their low-pitched mating boom was only heard by special people, the way mosquitos are only heard by young people, and thankfully Fran was neither.

Another boom, and she realised it was the fly screen on the front door. She snapped it locked and shut the main door behind it. It hadn't cooled much since dusk, so she switched on the fan in the living room and returned to the kitchen bench to cry — no, she didn't need to cry, she needed to ring Vincent, who would always be here for her.

★ ★ ★

She met Vincent at the insurance company when he invited her to his farewell party. Over the years, she'd moved around departments, eventually settling as a clerk in investments, the coolest division in the building, where suits played with money and had long, drunken lunches and sometimes got arrested for insider trading. The coffee was good and so was the staff room. There were doughnuts at 11.00 and drinks in South Melbourne at 6.00. The social club organised skiing trips and wine tours that were apparently a lot of fun. Fran liked the vibe of investments. It was interesting and happy, but not so much that work would ever bleed into her weekends 'with the boys' back home.

Then along came Vincent from sales. He'd only just joined the company, and was already leaving to study housing policy. The audacity of the guy. She was jealous.

Despite the brevity of his employment, everyone loved Vincent, and an elaborate and expensive farewell party was thrown by the social club. Fran and Vincent danced so hard they were dripping in sweat, and one or both of them thought it a good idea to go outside to cool down. Sometime after that they made the mistake of having sex — several times. Immediately realising they were not meant for each other in that way, they became best friends for nine months before becoming parents for the rest of their lives. They had lived and coparented together until twelve months ago, when their daughter scolded them for staying in all weekend, yet again:

'You're holding each other back,' Vonny said. 'You should both at least try and find your soul mate. What about passion, what about passion?!' Vonny was into true love. Her favourite movie was *The Princess Bride*.

Vincent moved to a terrace around the corner the following month. They'd since agreed to take turns to walk his dog, but often ended up doing it together. They shared disastrous dating stories (Vincent had been on three dates, all of them bad, while she'd been on seven, three of them good but only for a few hours). They texted and messaged each other all the time. They visited each other a little too much. It was all very grown up. It was easy to be grown up about falling out of love if you never fell in it.

Fran lifted the handset of the ancient mustard phone and pressed three buttons before realising she'd forgotten the rest of Vincent's mobile number. She hung up and thought hard for a moment before dialling again.

She was about to give up when a woman answered. 'Hello?'

'Oh hi, sorry. Is this 0491 570159?'

'Yeah, hi. Is that Fran? It's Constance here. Vinnie's told me so much about you.'

Vinnie? He hated being called Vinnie. As did Vonny, who vetoed it. 'There will be no rhymes in this family,' she had said.

Fran had heard nothing about *Constance* — stupid name. 'Is Vincent there?'

'He is. He's in the shower.'

Fran looked at the clock — 9.55 pm. Vincent never showered at this time. 'No, no, it's fine, just tell him I rang to say thanks for yesterday.' She hung up before Constance had finished her sentence and almost leaned into the desire to howl, stopping herself and heading to the desk, where she read over the day's log book and added various items to her various lists of things to do.

Gramps was making noises. She grabbed the log book, retrieved a bottle of pills from the chest in the cupboard, and headed to his bedroom.

'I don't like this, Franny,' he said, swallowing the pill she'd given him.

'It's sucky, isn't it?' Without thinking, she took her mother's rosary beads, which were hanging on the headboard, and held them in her father's hand. Her dad loved the rosary, but Fran hated it. Till tonight. It was soothing, chanty, and she was in a better mood by the time her dad fell asleep, which was during the second decade of the sorrowful mysteries — honestly, what a load of tosh.

She went to her old bedroom to get the bed ready for Vonny (who was the messiest person in the universe). The wall was still covered in posters of Kate Bush and The Proclaimers. Fran had been nuts about the Scottish duo at fifteen. It was liberating to realise there were other people out there with funny accents. Plus, The Proclaimers wore glasses and were twins, and twins were sexy, specially in glasses.

There was a huge space in the middle of the wall where her favourite Proclaimers and Kate Bush posters had once been, the only remnants being sticky-tape marks. The room needed a paint. The whole house needed a paint, she thought, as she walked back down the hall, adding it to her 'Household Maintenance' list of things to do.

Lights, gravel, The Captain was approaching. Fran checked herself in the bathroom mirror and opened the door.

'She's tipsy I'm afraid,' said The Captain, who was holding Vonny upright with his arm, his daughter Rosie just keeping it together behind them.

One day in this town and Vonny was pissed. Fran had never seen her in this state before.

'Mum! We found a room. I'm so sorry, my poor mum.' Vonny was talking gibberish — she'd found a room or a box or something.

'Shh, now,' Rosie said to her new friend, 'let's not talk about it till tomorrow, yeah, you and me? I'll come over first thing. I'm sorry Mrs Collins, we had some wine. It was all my idea. Is that all right, if I come over in the morning?'

'Sure.' This time, she did not insist on being called Fran.

'Maybe I could bring some tortilla,' said The Captain.

Rosie obviously didn't want it to be a family affair, and huffed back out to the car.

'Sorry about my daughter,' said The Captain.

Vonny, sprawled on the sofa, dry-retched loudly, and Fran thought it best to see her guests off. When she came back inside, Vonny had reached the spin and vomit stage. Hair-holding was required for a good hour.

'Never again,' said Vonny.

'But it's so fun for both of us,' said Fran, as her daughter heaved into the gross toilet bowl. She wouldn't even bother cleaning it. She'd buy and install a new one tomorrow. Remember to put it on the list, she said to herself, still holding her daughter's matted hair. Buy new loo.

Vonny wouldn't let her take her shoes or jeans

off. She was stubborn, even when paralytic, a word Fran shouldn't use now there was an actual paralytic person in the house.

She put a large bottle of water on the bedside table, a bucket beside the pillow, and began reading *The Faraway Tree* to her baby girl. The children had arrived in the Land of Topsy Turvy.

'I want to go to the Land of Do What You Want,' said Vonny, words fading.

'Isn't that the land you're already in?'

But Vonny had fallen asleep.

Fran unlaced her daughter's boots and put them on the window ledge. She hadn't seen these ones before; she must have borrowed them from Rosie. They were cute, cherry red Doctor Martens.

12

Nine Days Before the Fire

ROSIE

I shouldn't have bought these because they're made of animal, but I had to. I love them. They work with everything I own. I am never taking them off and I will always be thankful to the animal.

Doorbell. I'm busy, not gonna get it, someone else should get it, why is it always me who — ?

Someone got it.

It's decided: tonight I'm wearing the boots and this dress.

The little girls are kicking off at the door. 'Dad! DAD!' I put an apron over my outfit and head up the hall.

A woman is wielding a chainsaw at our door. She might rip the chord and kill me but I'm not scared about that, I'm scared about the girl she's with, her daughter I am told; another teenage fish left flapping in this town, who I am expected to *get* and befriend. Her name's Vonny and she's texting right in front of me with all her beeps still on, so I can't get away from the conversation she's having with her city pals, but I can't be part of it either. Thankfully her mother is wanting to drop the chainsaw and run.

'Fran! Fran Collins! Is that you?'

Dad knows the woman and is forcing fudge on her. Worse, he is forcing the daughter on me. He knows I know what he's thinking — that she should come to the dance with me tonight. But I don't want to babysit a girl who refuses to make eye contact with me — luckily, probably, because mine are angry. I try to stare Dad out, but he's practised this a lot, and wins.

The healthiest mint is in the veg garden at the end of Tragedy Track. I act as tour guide with the intention of repelling this Vonny girl. By the time I'm done, she won't want to go to the Blue Light Disco when Dad suggests it, and will therefore not ruin my evening.

'Granddad Brian had a heart attack in the old meat shed there,' I say to her. 'There are still hooks in the ceiling where he tried to make Dad slit throats. I'm the only one who goes in now. I've seen chains swinging, all by themselves. Twice I heard a man saying 'help'.' I ask her if she wants to go in, but she doesn't and we walk on. 'Dad's older brother, Uncle Martin, was supposed to shoot his sheep in that paddock,' I say. 'Shot himself instead.'

She's tearing up. She's overreacting. She didn't know Dad's brother.

I'm sorry about Uncle Martin, of course, but not as sorry as I am about the sheep. They moved north before I found out moving north was a euphemism. I'm telling her all this for some reason.

'There's a photo in the *Free Press* of four enormous trucks of fluff driving up the main street. People came out of shops to watch them leave, some men had hats and they put them against their chests.' Somewhere along the line she's lit a joint and I'm partaking. She's tricking me and it will not work.

'Better get the mint to Dad,' I say. We pick enough to last a year, and I up the pace down Tragedy Track. 'My horse died up there.' I point to McBean's Hill, and something about this Vonny girl's reaction causes me to get poetic: 'I saw Dad on his tractor. His hat against a sky that'd be a shepherd's delight most other places, red on a rolling hill. Something warmed me that hadn't done since Mum . . . Then I saw the rope attached. It was loose at first, and it ended somewhere over the hill. I was thinking a café would be nice on the top of that hill, just where that thing's coming from, when I realised Dad was dragging a dead horse. Mr McBean was heading north too.'

She's hugging me: 'You must never walk on this track ever again — find another route, go anywhere else, go on any other track.'

* * *

Back in the kitchen, something has changed. Vonny's mother just snort-laughed and is mimicking Dad's body language; one elbow on the table, legs crossed. My father is saying her name all the time — Fran, Francesca, Fran — and whatever happened between me and Vonny on Tragedy Track is eclipsed. Neither of us want our parents to flirt. We're both mad now. I don't want her to come to the dance, definitely not. And from Vonny's expression, she would rather stab herself in the eye than do dress-ups with little old me.

And yet, somehow, that's exactly what we end up doing.

★ ★ ★

I do have plenty of clothes, it's true. I've been gathering them from Op Shops on my city trips — mending, making adjustments, upscaling, and selling them online. So far I've raised $215, most of it from Maz and Ciara, the only cool people in town. 'I need another three hundred at least,' I say to Vonny, but I don't tell her what for and she doesn't ask (it's for a decent sewing machine). I've only known her an hour but it's already an on-off relationship.

She doesn't wear dresses, she tells me, so I take out the other boxes. She goes for a crop T-shirt with *MILK KILLS* written on it and says, 'Would this work with my jeans?'

Anything would work with her jeans.

'How much?'

If I charge her, we will just be friends. If I tell her the crop top is free, something might happen. 'Don't be daft,' I say, and she kisses my cheek.

'Oh my God, I know it's wrong but I love those!' She's wanting my cherry-red Doctor Martens boots, which are SO not for sale. I can't believe what I do — I tell her she can borrow them if she wants, even though I don't want her to borrow them. I don't want to ever take them off. She says, 'That'd be great!' and watches while I unlace them. It takes ages.

'I'll cherish them,' she says, 'and I'll give them back at the end of the night.'

They look better on her. I can't stop staring at them. I'm thinking about the cow that was skinned to make them. I can almost hear it squeal. I'm starting to think my boots have been stolen as punishment. By this girl. I fall in love easily, and have done it again. Which is perhaps why I choose a shorter dress than the one I'd picked out earlier, pairing it with home-knitted socks and Blundstone boots. I've been so unhappy, I've managed to reach size eight, and I look eighteen at least. I'm so hot, I can't imagine she thinks I'm not.

We have two hours till the disco and I have no idea how to fill it in this embarrassment of a madhouse. Dad's got classical music on — oh my God, Tchaikovsky — and the twins are harassing Vonny with questions they shouldn't be asking.

'My dad's Koori,' Vonny's saying to the brats, 'which means I am too.' She's being very kind to them. 'Yeah, they say my gran was stolen but it was much worse than stolen. She was playing in the front garden when some men grabbed her and put her in a car. She never saw her family again.'

The little girls are horrified, but distracted. 'What's the meanest thing anyone's ever said to you?' Harriet asks. 'Bridget O'Connor said I was a cross-eyed bitch the week before my birthday.'

Amy's got a better one: 'And Rosie said to me

76

that I shouldn't have children, and probably won't get to anyway, cos Australia's getting hotter and hotter and soon we're gonna be un-hab-able, and also city slickers are killing all the koalas.'

'Oh sweetheart,' Vonny says, giving Amy a hug, and exchanging suppressed smiles with Rosie. 'Um . . . it's not the meanest thing, but I don't like it when people ask how indigenous I am, like they want a percentage, or a certificate. No-one ever asks anyone else that. But actually I suppose I'd rather people asked stupid questions than didn't, long as they hang round to listen to the answer.'

Oh no, the little girls are about to ask a lot of stupid questions.

'So you're vegan?' I say, desperate to change the subject.

'I am, I'm vegan.'

She's giving me an odd look and I'm wondering if vegan is code. Hope so. I tell her 'I'm not a very good one. The Docs . . . and I had bacon and eggs in the city last Friday. Been thinking about it ever since.' The twins have gone for their tea, thankfully, and we are as dressed as we can be for the disco.

'What have you got to drink?' she says.

Dad banned booze in the house after Uncle Martin. We decide to grab the dinghy from her shed, which she calls The Shed of the Dead, and to sneak up into her brother's water tank. He hides weed in there. I have a stupid smile on my face and mustn't get too excited. Vonny, I prefer Veronica, might be indigenous, vegan, and from the city — but this does not mean she's into girls. We walk down Ryan's Lane towards her brother's house and I have my fingers crossed the whole entire time.

Vonny's brother is actually a half-brother and his dad is The Boarder. No-one likes to talk about The Boarder, including Dante, who's never met him, and who we spot kneading dough in the window of his shack. He looks too old to be anyone I know's half-brother, but Vonny assures me he is hers; borne out of a Blue Light Disco in 1989. 'We should be careful tonight,' she says.

I am fifty-two percent certain she is flirting with me.

Vonny found Dante's weed by accident, she tells me. The ladder up to the open-topped water tank is wonky and I'd rather not go up it. 'Throw it up,' she says, referring to the dinghy.

I toss up the lump of rubber and make a wish: *Please let me lie in this rubber boat and smoke all night.*

We take our boots and socks off and rest them on the top rung of the ladder. They look sweet together up there. There's only a foot of water in the tank and once we've inflated the dinghy we realise how much it stinks in here, weed mostly, but not entirely. Vonny's reaching for the ledge halfway up, which has an Esky cooler on it — Dante's stash. She rolls like an expert. We forget the smell for a while, and stare up at the circle of sky, which is a deep, getting-darker-every-second, blue. 'I'd kill for rain,' I say, and she turns my chin in order to kiss me.

78

This water tank is the best place in the whole entire universe.

13

The Day of the Fire

Fran removed the beanie but she couldn't see anything from the top of the monument, not at first. Smoke burned her eyes and caught her throat, made her double over coughing. She could hear horns and alarms and explosions and pop-pop-popping: gas bottles, she supposed. When it was safe to stand again, she saw that the smoke had cleared a little to the northwest and that something round was coming into view. Something tall. It was the water tank at Dante's. She scrambled for a one-dollar coin in her backpack, put it in the telescope, and homed in. There was something on the top rung of the ladder. It was hard to focus because she was shaking, and the water tank was at least three hundred metres away, but there was something on the top rung of the ladder, something red. Boots, it was a pair of boots; with melted heels dripping onto the steps below.

She ran down the spiral stairs, scraping and burning herself as she negotiated the tight bends through dense smoke. Vonny had those boots. She had them ten days ago, anyway. Fran had put them on the window sill in the bedroom. Had she seen them since? Yes, on Rosie, but they had swapped clothes again since then. Had they? Was Vonny wearing them this morning? What was Vonny wearing today?

She kicked the huge door at the bottom, but it didn't budge. Several kicks later, she gave up and made her way up to the lookout again, peering over to check the entrance.

Something large was obstructing the main door below. It took Fran a while to work out what it was because it was on fire.

An ostrich.

Ronnie Corbett?

Fran ran back down and pushed against the door with her back until it opened far enough for her to get out. She threw her blanket on his back, patted at the flames with her gloves, but it was too late. She wanted to cry over the bird's body, because she'd grown up with Ronnie Corbett, but also because he had got out. How? Had the fence burned? Yes, she told herself, the fence must have burned. Not the house. Her dad could still be alive. She couldn't breathe, and there was no time for crying. She did an involuntary sign of the cross for Ronnie Corbett and his unrequited love, Dame Miriam McDonald, who was faster than Ronnie. Maybe she'd made it.

Poor Ronnie. His death deserved to smell worse than barbecue.

She had to get to the water tank, which meant going back down the way she had come. From ground level, the Mountain Ash trees that lined the path were the only things visible in the thick black smoke. Ominous, giant burning devils, they were, trunks and limbs fizzing and spitting and firing their bark missiles. The town must

81

have been named after a fire in the early days of colonisation, but Fran didn't know the exact details, and neither did the *Encyclopaedia Britannica*.

The smoke would be opening their pods now, freeing their seeds. They were giving birth while everything else was dying. Destroy, Repair. Destroy, Repair.

A huge tree cracked and began to fall. Fran scrambled back inside the monument as it bounced and settled across the path. It wasn't safe outside, and there was no way she could get to the water tank the way she had come, via Ryan's Lane.

Back at the top of the lookout, the sky had cleared a little. She could see that the firestorm had cut a stripe through the town from the north-west to the south-east, as if a gigantic, fire-breathing bulldozer had ploughed through Ash Mountain, leaving nothing in its wake but thick smoke and demon-trees.

She looked through the telescope again, but her time had run out and she couldn't find another coin. She did a slow 360. There was a wriggly line of red-and-white lights extending well beyond the town in each direction. When one of the lights exploded, she realised she was looking at the old northern highway — North Road — crammed with evacuees, the closest of whom would surely be dead in their vehicles.

The back of the fire was roaring off towards unsuspecting towns in the south-east. What were the names of those villages exactly: Comrie, Brown Creek? To the north, the western side of the main street was on fire: was that the supermarket? The eastern side of North Road — including The Red Lion and the London Emporium and Gallagher's Bakery — was thus far unscathed. The wide main street, made for the hefty horse traffic between Melbourne and Sydney, had served the town again at last.

To the north-west, Ryan's Lane was still obscured by thick smoke, bar the water tank. It was clear now that the only way was if she ran down the eastern side of the hill, which was treeless, and circumnavigated the town, finding a route to Dante's via the college playing fields. She'd also be able to check the convent hall, as per the original plan. It was at the foot of the main street, beside the oval, and looked like it might have escaped the fire. Fran was supposed to meet Vonny at the convent at 4.00. And the oval was the place of last resort if the community siren went off. 'Please Vonny, be at the convent. Please be there, please be there,' she chanted as she raced down the hill.

And not in the water tank . . .

She mustn't think about the tank.

It would have been the heat, it would have been quick.

She mustn't think about the tank. Anyway, Vonny might have had runners on this morning. Would she wear runners with shorts? She was wearing shorts, Fran was almost sure. Fran had last been in the bedroom — When? Last night? — and they weren't on the window sill, were they? She couldn't remember if they were there.

There was hardly any water in that tank at

Dante's, it could have boiled, boiled.

Shh, she ran faster, changed her thinking —

Please not Vonny, please don't be Vonny, then stopped and vomited, because she knew what she was wishing for; that 'Please don't be Vonny' actually meant . . .

Please be Rosie.

PART TWO

THE OVAL

14

Thirty Years before the Fire

The Boarder liked what he was seeing and she was liking being it. Fran almost forgot about the dork dancing opposite her, who she'd escape as soon as the song ended.

'Another dance after this?' Brian Ryan Junior asked.

Oh Lord. 'Thanks, but I'm so thirsty.'

'Are you? Would you like a drink?'

'No, no, I don't, thanks.'

It took him a moment before finally getting the hint, and he crept off towards the men's toilets. She headed over to the bar area and was about to order a drink when . . .

'Want a drink?'

His accent! Could it be . . . ? He was Scottish!

She asked him a lot of questions and he liked that. He talked a lot. She could hardly understand him. His father worked between Melbourne and Singapore, he might have said, and dumped him here. He'd been playing cricket somewhere or other and had either won or lost.

She was glad he didn't ask her any questions. What on earth would she have said?

He was too cool to even bother to change out of his uniform for something as stupid as an Ash Mountain police-run reprobate kids' disco. He wore his shirt unbuttoned, had very white teeth and enough money in his wallet for a lifetime of lemonade. 'Lemonade, ta,' said Fran.

'No, I mean a *drink*.'

She should have asked what was in his flask, but she knew she was going to take a swig from it no matter — what with everyone, including Tricia Gallagher, watching and all. Fran was about to nab the coolest boarder in town. Christ, the stuff in his flask was like petrol.

Brian Ryan Junior was looking at her too. He was putting on his coat just as 'I'm on My Way' came on. The Proclaimers. Fran and The Boarder grabbed each other's hands at the same time — how about that, that meant something, did it not? — and raced to the floor. *A ha. A ha. A ha. A ha.*

It was so unfair, really, that The Boarder just happened to get the perfect song. Fran would never have followed anyone out the back after dancing to 'Kokomo' or 'Handle Me with Care', for example, but 'I'm on My Way' was a sign and it gave her courage. She was Sofia again, with a good dollop of perm-haired Olivia thrown in. She smiled at Tricia Gallagher, took another swig from The Boarder's flask, and followed him out the back door, from misery to happiness. A ha.

Uh-uh. The Boarder had completed his courting and his tongue was in her mouth. She didn't know if she liked it or not, but she didn't want to stop it. She was just really surprised they'd not talked beforehand, at all. Having had a few seconds to think, she now had quite a few things she thought she could say. When some local boys came out for a cigarette, he removed his tongue —

'Come, I know a special place.'

Two minutes later they were lying on the cricket pitch in the middle of the oval, staring up at the southern sky. Fran stopped herself from saying something about the stars or the universe and finished off the last drop of his petrol.

'As they say in the movies: isn't this romantic?' he said, rolling over for the type of grope she'd expect to happen several months later. She hardly realised what was occurring until she suddenly felt stuffed, literally, and a little sick. Can't have been more than two minutes when he rolled off again and did up his trousers.

A group of boys were walking along the main street. The Boarder stood and tucked himself in. 'I'd better go,' he said.

Her zip had broken. Her bra was twisted and stuck above her chest. If that was sex, she was going to find it very easy to avoid from now on. Her dad could sell the ostriches.

The Boarder had reached his clan on the main street — they were laughing. One yelled, 'Mountain Slut!'

It was true.

'Fran?'

A boy was behind her. She jumped up, prepared herself to run.

'I told your dad you were in the loo; we'd better hurry. Are you all right?'

She wasn't sure if she was all right, nor why she hugged Brian Ryan Junior and cried into his chest.

15

The Day of the Fire

There were at least twenty vehicles on the oval. Fran heard alarms and sirens in the distance, but there was no evidence of emergency services on the ground. The cars were all facing the same direction, like worshipping zombies. The ground cracked and ting-ed as she walked towards a Range Rover that had parked about five metres east of the oval. It was intact, engine off, keys in ignition, alarm blaring. So far, the town's safe meeting place appeared to have done its job. It was difficult to know for sure, though. The oval and all the cars were cloaked in smoke and ash. She knocked on the window of the Range Rover, expecting one of two outcomes: that the driver and/or passengers would unwind the window and say *Can you believe that fire?* Or that there would be no-one in the car because everyone had taken refuge in a building nearby — the convent, for instance, which had escaped harm by the looks, and where Vonny was supposed to be. There was no response, so Fran wiped the glass with her jumper. The vehicle was empty.

An hour ago, Fran would have said she'd suffered a great deal of trauma. Her mother had been run over on Fran's fifth day at Prep. She got pregnant at fifteen. Her father had a stroke. And Vincent was someone else's best friend now.

But as she weaved her way through the vehicles on the oval, she saw something that trumped all those other traumas put together. The cars at the western edge were burnt out, many were on fire, and not all of them were empty. The hatchback, for example, which she should not have stopped beside, and definitely should not have looked inside. In the front there were — one, oh God, two — in the back — one, two, a car seat between. A family of five, charred. Who had three little ones? Who had a hatchback?

She ran.

The convent was difficult to access from North Road, which was strewn with crashed vehicles, but she managed to make it to the double doors.

The hall had been abandoned mid-fete. The spinning wheel had stopped at Lose a Turn. The Best Knitted Cat had gone to Lena Kamiński.

16

Nine days before the fire

ROSIE

We're late and stoned, and I decide we should go into the hall holding hands. I'm pretending to be the cool one when Vonny's thinking nothing of it and I'm scared shitless. Sure enough, the group of boarders in the foyer make comments and laugh, and several people stare as we make our way to the dance floor, but after that, nothing much happens. Homophobia is a little tired here tonight. I'm half relieved and half disappointed because, with Vonny holding my hand, I wouldn't have cared about any abuse, and I've been longing to not care.

The dance is dire, anyhow. Two couples are groping on the seats near the stage, a DJ is playing ancient rock, and no-one is dancing but us. We do our best to Ballroom Blitz it, then I suggest we break into the kitchen and get some alcohol. Everyone knows Sister Mary Margaret is a lush. There'll definitely be wine there, maybe vodka.

'Is she the ancient one?' Vonny asks.

'Last one standing.'

'Mum finished off form five here. Sister Mary Margaret was her private teacher, and the school nurse.' Vonny is totally up for stealing

92

from this particular nun.

I lead her from the seventies hall extension, to the older part of the enormous rambling gothic bluestone building which, as far as I know, is home to one drunk nun.

We're in the central hall, which has a big, square staircase in the middle. Everything's made of wood and smells of sorrow and there are two ghosts staring at me. 'Holy shit.'

'They're just pictures on the wall,' Vonny assures me. 'Mary and Ned, see?'

She's pointing the torch on her phone at Mary, who is scary, and then at the masked robber, who's not. 'Phew, thanks,' I say.

There must be ten rooms on the first floor and I hope the nun's asleep in one of them.

A door slams, upstairs. I hold back a scream but Vonny doesn't manage. We sprint together, past the living room, down a dark, tiled corridor, and into the kitchen, hiding under the table as footsteps approach.

The top half of the door is glass and is darkening with a shadow that's turning into something — a face, Sister Mary Margaret's, scraggly grey-white round the edges, withered and hateful. I'd have preferred to see the teeth of an actual dinosaur. Vonny and I scramble backwards as quietly as we can, opening a door and locking ourselves in behind it.

The nun's come in to the kitchen. I hear her switch on the light, checking the back door, walking from one end of the kitchen to the other. At last, the door shuts.

Vonny turns the light on and we realise we're

in the old sick room. There's a hospital bed in the middle, which Vonny lies on. She closes her eyes.

There's a window between the rooms, with metal Venetian blinds covering them. I walk through the door to the adjoining room and I'm surprised to see there's a desk on the other side. There is also a really comfy chair; tweed, orange, goes up and down, swivels. Behind the desk is a metal cabinet. In front of the desk are the blinds. I separate two of the blinds and peek into the other half of the room. 'I can see you!' I say to Vonny, who may have fallen asleep on the sick-bay bed.

We agree it's a good idea to down the rest of the cask of Rosé in the old nun's fridge, and to have a squiz in the cabinet behind the desk.

It's mostly home to bills and other boring stuff, but one file has clippings in it about how the parish was cleaning up its act after the 'scandal' in the eighties. Father Frank, barely in his thirties at the time, was staying on to resurrect the parish, according to the *Ash Mountain Free Press*. He gave good apology, young Father Frank. He used good words, like sorry.

'He hasn't got any better-looking,' I say. When not in ludicrous robes, he wears the right jeans and the right T-shirt but in the wrong way to the power of ten. He must iron for hours. His hair's like a wig; maybe it is. Worst of all, he's a lip-kisser. There are a lot of lip-kissers among the oldies in these parts — for example, Mrs O'Leary and Aunty Cathy and Uncle Dan. It's downright dirty in my opinion, especially for a fifty-year-old priest. No-one kisses on the lips in the inner city unless it's sexual, especially not priests, although I never knew one in the city.

'My gramps adores Father Frank,' says Vonny.

She's found something underneath the cabinet and is making a racket trying to move the whole entire thing. She's managed to slide the cabinet away from the wall. Underneath is a large hatch with a lock, which she's picking at with a hair clip. She's too sexy doing this, I'm thinking, then she ruins everything with:

'I reckon your dad fancies my mum.'

'I know,' I say, even though it's totally the other way around. Every woman in town fancies my dad, and every single one of them, especially Vonny's mum, can fuck right off.

She's unlocked the hatch and it's now opening, slowly. It might not be creaking, but I feel it's creaking. It's certainly the type of slow-opening secret hatch you would expect to creak. Whatever, a creak manifests and is gone when Vonny finds a light switch.

A staircase, which we head down, of course, chemically confused idiots that we are. It leads to a stone wine cellar, which is lined floor to ceiling with thick wooden shelves. I take a selfie, my first of the night, and I am hoping I will get a chance to take some more. We look amazing together. On the shelves behind us are some small boxes of different shapes and sizes, each covered in cuttings from magazines and posters — there's a floral one, a Barbie one, The First Eleven and The Ashes, *Thomas the Tank Engine*, Essendon

Football Team, David Essex, Kate Bush and The Proclaimers, Cars, Dora the Explorer.

I look in the Dora one, which has *ELLIE 5,* written on top, but it's empty bar a piece of paper with *IOU* written on it.

Vonny reaches for the hatbox covered in pictures of Kate Bush and The Proclaimers. 'Thought so,' she says, looking on the lid.

FRANCESCA 15 — is written in black capitals.

17

Eight Days before the Fire

'Wakey, wakey, Mum . . . '

Vonny was up without argument for the first time ever. Her hair was wet. Was that mascara? 'Have you made proper coffee?' Something was wrong.

'Rosie and her dad'll be here in ten minutes. Quick!'

Fran had last checked on her dad at 5.30 am and he was upset. They both were. He was sleeping now. The nurse would arrive at nine, half an hour. She had no time for breakfast with the neighbour, even if he was hot, which he probably wouldn't be this early in the morning; he'd probably look as rough as she did — did she look rough? She should check.

She found herself hoping that her dad stayed asleep until she'd at least had a coffee when the doorbell rang. She dashed along the hall — 'Vonny, wait!' — but didn't make it to the pawprint room. When Vonny opened the door, she bolted into Dante's old room.

Sometimes she hated her daughter.

'Hello. Oh wow, that smells amazing,' Vonny was saying.

There was no way to get to her clothes without being spotted. Fran looked through Dante's cupboard and managed to find a pair of old

97

shorts that fit. She hand-ironed Vincent's fraying *Tiddas* T-shirt, put her hair up, slapped colour into her cheeks, and headed towards the tortilla.

★   ★   ★

It was the oddest breakfast: two polite couples at a deadly dinner party, and The Captain did not look rough. There was too much light in this room altogether, and Fran's calf hairs were glistening below her son's camouflage shorts. 'You going to the ten-thirty? I heard from a very cute source that you didn't believe in all that.'

'Cathy?'

'Adorable and terrifying.'

'Exactly! Yeah, no, we've got a wedding at twelve — Rosie set out my clothes for me.'

Light chinos and a farmer's shirt with just the right number of undone buttons (two). 'Well done, Rosie.'

'Thanks,' Rosie said.

'Mr and Mrs Bevowik from Upper Templestowe,' said The Captain to the group. 'They're having the ceremony on our hill.'

'They're planting trees as vows,' said Rosie. 'We had to buy matching shovels.'

'The earth's hard as rock up there,' said The Captain.

'It's gonna be so funny,' said Rosie. 'It's concrete.'

Fran had banter with her daughter, too, sure she did; she had a great relationship with Vonny. Um: 'We think weddings are sadder than funerals.'

'We as in you and me?' said Vonny.

Well yes! Vonny had said she totally thought this too — when was it? — right enough it was probably a good few years ago. She might have been as young as ten, the golden age when everything Fran did was funny and clever and amazing. That had stopped suddenly, along with Vonny wanting to do any of the things they used to do; like walking to the Old Reservoir and back; and eating out in the city. Fran's friends at work, who'd brought up kids, assured her it was just typical teenage behaviour, but Fran was always worried it was more than that. 'Everyone thinks I stole Vonny,' she said.

'Mum!'

'People look at me that way, when her dad's not around, which will be all the time now. I didn't steal her.'

'That's good,' said The Captain.

'Wanna see the ostriches?' Vonny stood, desperate to get away, and it didn't take much to convince Rosie.

Fran was alone with The Captain. 'I hear it's gonna hot up.' She could easily keep the weather going till Nurse Jen arrived. It wasn't small talk to country folk. But The Captain had something else on his mind.

'The girls have left us alone so I can tell you something.'

She liked that he didn't pause before saying what.

'They broke into the convent last night and found some photos of you in the wine cellar. Here.' He slid three pieces of paper across the

99

table, then turned his face away. 'I only saw them once, like a glance, then . . . I haven't looked since . . . Not that they're . . . Well, you have a look.'

The first was a photo of her in the sick room at fifteen, her bump not showing yet. She was standing against the height bar on the wall, dressed only in her yellowing ill-fitting bra and undies. It wasn't a happy time — she certainly wasn't smiling — but it wasn't sinister. The second and third were similar: one on the sick bed, one on the chair — again, dressed only in her bra and undies. 'I don't understand,' said Fran.

'They were in the wine cellar,' said The Captain. 'It's under the office next to the sick room. Vonny spotted a hatbox with Kate Bush on it.'

'And The Proclaimers,' Vonny said. She and Rosie had not been with the ostriches, but listening at the door.

Fran still didn't understand. 'Sister Mary Margaret taught me there for the second half of fifth year. I had private checkups in the sick bay because I refused to go to the surgery. What are you on about? Is that Gramps waking?'

'No,' said Vonny. 'He's sound asleep. I just checked.' She and Rosie returned to the table, and Vonny put one of the photos in the middle.

The Captain looked away.

'Why are you looking away? There's nothing to look away from,' Fran said.

'One photo isn't weird,' said Vonny, putting the second on the table. 'Two, not so weird either.'

Everyone but The Captain was looking at the third now, also of a vulnerable pregnant teenager in her underwear, and it was starting to be weird.

'We got scared so we only saw these, but there we think there were lots more in the hatbox, Mum.'

Fran needed to make a fresh pot of coffee, urgently. 'Um, so, that is weird. I don't know how to feel. Who's wanting a top-up?' As she filled the percolator, she spotted The Captain turning the photos over, trying to slide them off the table and get them out of sight. 'I'll keep those.' She snatched them and slammed them face down on the bench beside the stove.

'I'm sorry,' he said. 'Rosie came to me because she didn't know what to do . . . To be honest, I didn't know what to do either. The plan was that I'd talk to you privately.'

She had lifted the lid on the percolator and was watching the coffee rise. 'I do — I know what to do, it's fine.' The coffee maker was spitting hot syrup onto the back of the photos. She should shut the lid, turn the gas off, both. 'Hang on.' She snapped the lid and turned off the gas. 'You broke into the convent?'

Vonny was good at thinking on her feet. 'We just walked into the convent through the side door. Oh my God, Rosie, your boots! I forgot to give your boots back! We did break into the wine cellar, but we locked it up again; no-one will ever know.' And off they ran.

That was Nurse Jen knocking on the door. The Captain followed her and whispered, 'What are you going to do?'

101

'Sorry?'

'About the photos. You said you know what you're going to do.'

Nurse Jen was ringing the bell now. And her dad was moaning. She had to get The Captain out. 'Two things: I'm going to ask the nun to give me the box back without landing the girls in deep shit, if that's okay with you. Rosie'd probably get a warning; for Vonny it'd be jail and she'll probably never get out. Second: I'm going to avoid you. You're a jinx. I'm that girl again?' Fran pointed to the splattered photos beside the cooker. 'I'm her?' The nurse was ringing and her dad was calling her name and she was thinking about crying. 'I'm upset, but it's fine, I know what to do and now you do too.' She let Nurse Jen in, The Captain out, and shut the door.

Oops, Rosie was still inside. 'Bye Mrs Collins,' she said, pushing past.

And Fran watched the girl in the cherry-red boots walk towards her father's forgettable car.

★ ★ ★

Vonny was in bed with a sore head, and Nurse Jen was in charge of Gramps for the next four hours, which meant Fran could do anything she wanted. She opened the windows and doors, but there was no breeze. She turned on the television, *The Love House*, turned it off again. Everything was icky, the world was yucky, the light was bad. She splashed her face with a tiny amount of water and closed herself in the bedroom to ring Vincent. 'What's she got that I haven't, this Chelsea person?' she said.

'Constance.'

'Right.'

'She's very nice, and don't worry, she's not jealous of you at all.'

'That's . . . I'm just ringing to say I'll put Vonny on the three-thirty.'

'Cool. You okay?'

'I am.'

'Love you F Face, talk soon.'

Fran had called to tell Vincent everything, but he wasn't her listener anymore.

She changed into her running gear as quickly as she could and sweated it out along Ryan's Lane, up and over the monument track, and along North Road. She jumped the fence across from St Michael's onto the old railway land. It was her favourite run, down that hill, along those long disused lines, then up to The Tree.

It was a large oak, and was on the hill beside the Old Reservoir. Gramps had proposed to her mum here, and the two of them had made plans for a new life in the country. Apparently, Sofia said this was the most beautiful view she'd ever seen — and her family was from Tuscany.

She remembered Gramps bringing her here when she was five, both of them dressed in black, shoes off, feet in the water.

'Stuff happens,' he'd said, fishing rod in hand. 'Things get interrupted.'

Fran was crying her eyes out. 'But no, no, no, what are we supposed to do now?'

'Have a cry, then make new plans,' he'd said.

He brought her here at sixteen too, quite a few

times that year, baby Dante in a pouch on his chest, a fishing rod in his hand, Fran usually crying.

And when she was thirty, pregnant, lying down, sighing; her fourteen-year-old son holding a fishing rod beside his beloved Grandpa.

★   ★   ★

Fran headed back down the hill and onto the railway tracks, sprinting all the way to the oval, where she stopped to stretch.

Sunday lunchtime downtown Ash Mountain: the oval was littered with last night's bottles and cigarette butts, the soon-to-be-replaced statue of Bert Gallagher had been vomited on by someone who had cancer or had eaten tandoori. The Red Lion carpark was crammed with the vehicles of families having counter meals of chicken parmigiana and peppercorn steak.

Fran was hungry.

A group of young men with a boat named *Red Rocket* were getting snacks at Gallagher's Bakery, on their way to Lake Eildon, probably. And the convent was . . . the convent was right in front of her. One last stretch and she headed that way.

★   ★   ★

Fran expected the elderly nun to take ages to answer the door — the building was an enormous bluestone rectangle with a hall attached — and it was a shock when Sister Mary

Margaret appeared almost immediately.

'Hello?'

'Hello! Sister Mary Margaret, do you remember me? I'm Fran Collins — Francesca.' The same Sidney Nolan was still hanging in the hall, and that was about as welcoming as the place would get. 'You taught me when I was pregnant. Do you remember Little Dante? Sorry, I've just been running.'

'*Little* Dante? He's enormous! Course I know him. His half-acre feeds me, practically — come look at his miracles. *Francesca*. Come, come, I was just about to pop on the kettle.'

The zucchini on the kitchen table were impressive — Dante had a knack for enabling things to take off.

'I can't stay for tea, sorry. I've got to get back to Dad.'

'Would you like something other than tea?'

'Um, maybe water, thanks.'

Poor Sister Mary Margaret, the lonesome lush. She poured Fran's water first, then — 'It's five o'clock somewhere' — squeezed herself a reasonable-sized glass of cask rosé, plopping two round ice cubes in it. 'I made toffee!' It was in a lovely tin. Sister Mary Margaret was into pretty containers. This one had cows on it. 'I'd love to be able to chew it. I can only suck it these days. Take some.' Sister Mary Margaret put a small piece of toffee in the side of her mouth and did not chew it. 'Your dad — how's your dad?'

'Terrible.' Fran's speech had been disabled by the toffee. 'No, he's okay. He can't move, or do anything. He wants to die.'

'I'll try and get out this week, do some crosswords with him.' Sister Mary Margaret had shrunk a tad, but still towered over Fran at eighty-something. She used to have a kind face. Fran would describe it as sad now — that made two of them — but not unkind. She lit a cigarette and opened the kitchen window.

Fran wanted one badly. She could also murder a glass of wine. She took the toffee out of her mouth. 'I remember I had a hatbox when I was here, for my own special things. You called it a 'treasure box' and said it would always be here for me. I decorated it with posters of Kate Bush and The Proclaimers. I was wondering if you still have it.'

The nun butted out her fag and refilled her glass with rosé. 'I doubt it. So long ago. The things we used to say to children!'

'Of course, you probably threw it out. Just I kept crafty things in mine that I'd like to have, and some photos. It could be in the sick bay.' Fran looked at the half-glassed door adjoining the kitchen. 'Just in there.'

Sister Mary Margaret took her iPhone out from under her habit and handed it to Fran. 'Give me your number and I'll have a look later, you mind? That was me right in the middle of a show.'

'Oh sorry, what are you watching?'

'Housewives.'

The nun's tone intimidated Fran.

'Of New York.'

Fran left immediately.

⋆ ⋆ ⋆

106

The Red Lion was mobbed for a Sunday at 9.00. There'd been cricket all day at the college, according to Henry Gallagher, and the fete committee and a few Lions had wound up at the bar after their working bees. Dante made her come. He was forcing her to get out of the house every Sunday after the Old Mill closed, 9.00–11.00, there were to be no objections.

Where the hell was she supposed to go at that time in Ash Mountain? She brought the buggy with Gramps on a Stick, who was as reluctant as she was, and the iPad was head-height beside her at the bar. Three shots of sambuca sat in front of Gramps. The barman — Bert Gallagher's grandson, Pete — was pouring him a fourth, which was on Marti Ercolini and his wife and his son-in-law, all three huge fans of the way the chemist *used* to be run.

It was pretty clear that Dante and Gramps were having a dooby at home. They were giggly. 'Turn the monitor left a tad, can you Pete?' Gramps asked the barman. 'Down a bit, up, stop!'

The screen was now pointing at fifty-something Mrs Verity O'Leary's cleavage, which was hefty.

Fran wheeled the buggy over to Verity's table. 'Dad's wanting to say hello!'

He tried to object en route — 'Fran, Francesca!' — but it was no use, his head was opposite Verity's. 'How's that nasty rash?' he asked her.

Verity, cleavage well out of view, had terrible teeth and yellow eyeballs and indeed looked as if

107

she might have several nasty rashes. 'Matthew Collins, is that you . . . Are you still there?' A puff of smoke had clouded the screen. 'Matthew?' The monitor went black.

Fran, back at the bar with her white wine and quick crossword, had decided she should give up and head home, when The Captain came in, bringing a breeze with him. There was silence in The Red Lion for a country-and-western moment, then The Captain moved; heading straight for the stool beside Fran. She slid one of Gramps' sambucas his way. 'It's not gonna be easy avoiding you, is it?'

'I was dropping some guests here, they're staying upstairs.'

Two women in ridiculous hats had settled at the other end of the bar.

'How was the wedding?'

'Beautiful. She had great hair. He was a dick.'

He hadn't downed his sambuca. 'Are you driving?'

'I'm forty-seven.'

'And?'

'It's dark.'

'These are gonna go to waste.' Fran moved a second sambuca his way and downed one herself, gesturing Pete for another round. 'I hate this town. It's a serial-abused serial-abuser.'

The Captain took a shot and looked round the room. Three adult Ercolinis were playing darts. The Lions were telling jokes. The fete committee had merged with the wedding guests and were toasting the absent bride and groom with a round of actual champagne, and Verity O'Leary was trying to turn on Gramps on a Stick.

'If you hate where you came from, then likely you hate yourself,' said The Captain.

'Really, *Confucius* . . . ?' What rubbish. How could she hate herself when she was always so busy? 'Why do you let people call you The Captain? Are you not embarrassed?'

'If someone nicknamed you after a Jane Fonda character and it stuck, would you object?'

'I'm not ready to be Grace.'

'I was going to say Barbarella.'

'Pleased to meet you, The Captain.' Fran extended her hand.

He shook it. 'You're gonna love this town, Babs.'

★   ★   ★

An hour later, Fran and The Captain rolled out of the bar wheeling the buggy with Gramps on a Stick, the monitor still blank.

'It's better lit via the playing fields,' said The Captain, who was making a lot of health-and-safety related decisions.

She was wearing his jumper, drinking a bottle of water, and had just promised she would not beg the teenagers out front for a cigarette. They both had one and they were wasting them tongue wrestling by the side of the bakery. Fran readied herself to make a plea.

'Do not even think about it,' said The Captain.

They crossed the road. On the pavement ahead was The Spot. The Captain might not realise where they were, he may never have seen the flowers her dad left there for ten years, which Fran always retrieved and composted well before death. The Captain might stand on it, he might say something, make her talk about it when she did not want to.

He didn't, he moved to the right; he knew. She was only five, but she remembered BR Junior was at her mum's funeral with his family, and that he cried more than she did. Against the advice of everyone, her dad had taken her to the funeral. She was glad, as she'd been there to stop him jumping in the grave.

She and The Captain walked past The Spot. She said nothing. He said nothing. For at least twelve steps they walked in companionable silence, each knowing the other was thinking about heartbreak and therefore feeling the worst of it all at once, all over again. He was a decent chap, this Captain, but The Spot etcetera had caused her buzz to wane and she was about as ready for that as she was to be eighty-year-old Jane Fonda, as fabulous as she was.

'Race you to the gates,' she said, abandoning Gramps on a Stick and bolting off towards the college for five strides.

He didn't realise she'd stopped, and she found it less funny the further along he raced. He wasn't a running machine. Maybe because he was drunk. His legs were spindly, his left hand all over the place. She shouldn't have tricked him. Even with the buggy she would totally have won.

★ ★ ★

110

The college was as pretty as Oxford, probably. She'd never been to Oxford, or England, or anywhere, but she loved Inspector Morse and — she did not really like this about herself — pretty much anything that was on the BBC. The college, built in 1901, had ornate iron gates and a long driveway lined with oak trees that should never have been planted here. She loved this avenue — even though it led you to the college, where her life ended. It was glorious, especially as a kid in summer, as it had the only decent shade for acres and wound up at the school pool, which you could swim in for free during the holidays if you didn't mind getting felt up. Fran and Tricia didn't mind at all when they were six. Every day all summer they joined a queue of girls under twelve who didn't mind. It was so fun to be twirled in the water by Mr Brown or/and Brother Colin, one big hand gripping the in-between in order to power the twirl, so fun.

The main building was red with white trimmings, an ornate veranda thrown in to say *Yes, it's as if we're in Kensington, but we also have sunshine.* It was pretty, unlike bluestone St Michael's next door, the first Catholic church to be built outside of Melbourne and even less welcoming than the jail.

'They dumped their shit here and they're still doing it,' said Fran, walking through the stone-arched quadrangle and then onto the perfect lawn no-one was allowed to walk on — there were signs. 'Another infection that didn't quite manage to destroy.' She had crossed

111

to the other side of the quadrangle and reached the dorms. She pressed her face against the wall. 'I smell abused children. '*Please Father, I don't want to go into the projector room; please, I don't want to be a projector-room boy.*' She was very drunk, and slid down to rest with her back against the wall. 'It's like that song, the Court of King Caractacus . . . 'Oh the priest who raped the nun and touched the boy who fucked the slut of Ash Mountain'.'

The Captain was now sitting on the ground beside her. 'You do know whose song that is, 'The Court of King Caractacus'?'

She thought for one second. 'No?'

'B side to 'Two Little Boys'.'

Everything *was* icky. 'I don't want to talk about the hatbox,' she said.

'Okay.'

'I don't have to talk about it; no need to.'

'No.'

'I don't remember anything weird, I don't remember photos being taken. If a nun wanked over them, so what? Did it harm me? If I was abused and I don't know, would it help me to know? What's the difference between this situation and posting something on Instagram?'

'A lot.'

'If someone's abused in the bush and there's no-one there to hear it . . . '

'It still happened . . . Sorry, it's just, my little girls are still growing up in this town.'

Footsteps, a dark figure — it was Father Frank, walking on the other side of the quadrangle. They rose in synch, raced past the pool and across the footy fields towards the northern grandstand.

'They're smoking!' Fran had spotted two boarders on the top bench, and was running up the stairs and along the aisle. 'Hey boys, spare a smoke?' She must have been pissed. Boarders usually scared the shit out of her. In fact, these two could be the ones from the monument, who'd called Vonny a Mountain Slut. She hadn't seen their faces yet, but if it was them she was ready. 'Or are you complete arseholes?' she said.

The Captain remained at ground level. 'Fran! Come down!'

They were not Boarders #1, #2 and #3 from the monument, but two entirely fresh ones.

'He's an arsehole,' said Boarder #4. 'Whereas I'm lovely.' He lit a fag and handed it to her. He had droopy blue eyes, a blond aristocratic flop of hair and slobbery always-open lips that indicated a nasal problem of some sort and which had drowned the end of the cigarette. He also had good legs.

The Captain had arrived on the top level, panting. 'You shouldn't be smoking up here boys, you're one huge pile of kindle.'

'Lighten up, The Captain,' Fran said, exhaling.

'This valley's a tinderbox and this grandstand is a firelighter,' he said. 'Hi, I'm Brian, from the farm.'

Brian from the farm. Mmm. 'Why are you two stuck here during the summer?' she asked.

'We're orphans,' said Boarder #5, straight lined and revved for a dance or a fuck or a fight, whichever was on offer first. 'Will you be my mummy?'

'We're doing resits,' said Boarder #4. 'Want to take one for the road?'

'Thanks boys but I don't smoke,' said Fran, butting out her cigarette and following The Captain back down. They'd almost reached the ostrich fence when one of the boarders yelled.

'MILFO!'

Fran heard MILF and smiled. Perhaps she was wrong about boarders.

'Mum I'd Like to Fuck Off!' yelled the other.

Nup, they were all arseholes.

18

The Day of the Fire

FROG

Adam is Smithy to his friends, the very best of whom is me. I'm Frog. We are spitting from the top bench of the grandstand. Smithy is winning — his gob landed on the second bench from ground level. It is very impressive.

I stole a watering can from the college greenhouse and spray Smithy's legs — he's wearing board shorts — and then mine. He's lying on the second top bench now, I'm on the top. We're alone here, fifty feet in the air, legs wet for a split second then dry again. We went to Smithy's mum's house in Preston but she has a new boyfriend and he wouldn't let Smithy have his own bungalow to himself so we snuck back to Mounty again, figuring there'd be some local tarts on the loose. It's so hot that we've been in and out of the pool since getting back, no sign of any pussy but the pussy round here is gross anyhow, can't believe we chase it all the time.

'It's gone so quiet,' says Smithy.

'Yeah.' The sky looks strange too, dark. I light two fags and hand one to Smithy. 'I bet the whole town's quiet. We should go to the bottle shop.'

'Pool first?'

'Then bottle shop.'

Smithy sits up to enjoy the last few drags of his cigarette. His hair's moving — there must be a cool change, oh please.

Before I know what to make of it, the sky's bright red and there's a terrible noise, as if a plane's about to smash into us.

'Is that an ostrich?'

There's a dinosaur bolting across the oval. We are both standing on our respective benches now. Smithy has dropped his cigarette onto my bench and I can't stop looking at it. I'm about to lean down and put it out but the heat and the noise makes me turn around. The sky behind us is on fire, missiles are shooting the grandstand, and a wall of flames is heading straight for us.

These two benches will not lead us anywhere. We're running along them anyway.

19

Six Days before the Fire

Fran was getting into some necessary and depressing routines. She was up every three hours with her dad during the night, had her biggest meal (pre-prepared by Dante) at 10.00 am, including a glass of dusty sherry, and dozed whenever she could in the afternoon. She was on the sofa at 3.20 when the doorbell rang. She checked on her dad, who was still sleeping with the television on in the background — (The Love Housers were doing an obstacle course involving tarantulas and key lime pies). She switched it off and answered the door.

It was Father Frank, and he was carrying a large, reusable plastic bag. 'Francesca, top of the afternoon to you.' He didn't wait for her to invite him in, and she just let it happen. He had vampire qualities. He put the bag on the kitchen bench. 'Sister Mary Margaret asked me to drop this bag off, didn't say what's in it.'

Fran wanted to look inside the bag, but didn't. 'Great, thanks.' There might have been an awkward pause, Fran wasn't sure. 'Cup of tea?'

'Love one, thank you. Is he up for a visit?'

'Sorry, he's asleep. You have it the same as Dad, right?'

The tea-making distracted her and the priest was on his way up the hall to her dad's bedroom.

'Father?'

'Just looking in on him,' he said.

He'd definitely be awake now. Fran completed her father's tea routine (hers too, now) and carried the cup and saucer to the bedroom. She could hear something before she went in, but she wasn't sure what it was till she saw it. Her dad was sobbing loudly. Father Frank was holding him, his head buried into the invalid's chest. Fran put the tea on the bedside table and returned to the kitchen.

She listened to the sobbing for ages, then there was silence for a while, then the sh-sh-sh-shushing of the rosary, which was going on for ever. She tried to block out the noise by concentrating on today's project at her desk, an Invasion Day poster for Vonny's protest at the fete. So far it was colourful and informative, but not at all eye-catching. It needed work. Vonny hadn't shown any interest in holding a protest at the fete, but Fran thought she'd make the poster just in case she changed her mind. Vonny often changed her mind. She also did one hell of a protest. Thankfully, Nurse Jen arrived just as Father Frank exited her dad's bedroom. Fran said goodbye to the priest, did the handover and log book with Nurse Jen, and closed herself in the bedroom to look in the bag.

Sister Mary Margaret had responsibility for all the sick Catholic school children in town. She set up a crafts area in the kitchen, and among other projects designed to keep the meek meeker, encouraged her patients to make a 'treasure box' while they waited for their mothers and fathers to collect them. In the box, the nun put each child's favourite lollies and any precious artwork they created. Fran remembered slapping bits of posters she loved on a hatbox, then regretting it, as she was not allowed to take it home. She recalled a young boy with asthma — he was so pale and broken. What was his name . . . Johnny? He took a great deal more care with his, if she remembered correctly, sticking perfectly cut pictures of unusual insects on his sad shoebox, wheezing all the while.

That sadness was flooding her again as she took the hatbox out of the bag and lifted the lid.

There were no photos inside, just a thirty-year-old Choo Choo Bar (her dad had banned these in every part of the house bar the bath, and he only allowed this once), and three drawings of angry-looking apples. She flung the box onto the bed and called Vonny. 'So I got my box back, and there are no photos.'

'Oh my God, then there's definitely something dodgy. You need to call the police.'

Vonny was always such a drama queen. Anyway, she was paralytic that night. 'Are you sure there were more photos?'

'Yes.'

Fran still didn't trust her. Even if she did, she'd probably be able to let it go. 'What about the other boxes? You said there were more.'

'I only looked in another couple. There was nothing in those . . . Oh, one had a piece of paper with IOU written on it.'

'How many boxes were there altogether?'

'Let me think.'

119

Vonny was either thinking or lighting a fag. Her answer would make all the difference. One out of three boxes thus far contained at least three photographs of a near-naked youth. If Vonny's answer was five — that there were only another two treasure boxes in the cellar — Fran would take no further action. It was all about the odds.

'I'd say dozens,' Vonny said.

★ ★ ★

Fran stopped short of The Captain's — he was not the right person to talk to. Maz, originally a Yorkshire lass, had been a city prosecutor till trees and kids enticed her away — her Golf was in her drive — perfect. Fran needed a logical mind.

'Franchy, get in quick before he gets out.' Maz was referring to her youngest son, Ned, three, who almost got out. She had something crusty on her cheek, and her modern glassy pad was a complete mess. 'Luca, get your face out of the Bolognese.' Luca, seven, did not comply and continued holding his breath in the bowl.

It was 6.00 pm, and Maz's mind was anything but logical. The boys were still on school holidays, and Ciara was working stupid city hours.

'We've given up trying to sell,' she said, lifting Luca's head out of his bowl. (He took a huge breath.)

'We might rent something in the city for Ciara. We're asleep when she gets home anyway. Glass of red?'

'I should have thought about what time it is. Should I leave you? Or help?' Fran said.

'You can help by providing adult conversation.'

'That's why I'm here actually — let's settle the boys first.'

The boys were now throwing spaghetti at each other. It took two women five minutes to get them wiped and cross-legged on the floor. *Thomas the Tank Engine* and Neapolitan ice-cream in cones should also get a mention.

Wine poured, and Maz was logical again. She had her reading glasses on, and was using a magnifying glass to examine the three photos. 'The nun's in the room with you — see?'

There was a splodge of black and white behind Fran's left shoulder. With the magnifying glass, Fran could see a tiny section of nun habit. No big deal. She was the nurse.

'But she didn't take the photos. And if you don't know who did, maybe you didn't know they were being taken.'

Maz pointed to the mirror behind young Fran in the photo, then zoomed in on the Venetian blinds that were reflected in them. Fran could now see that two of the slats were separated by about an inch. 'I'd say the photographer was on the other side of the glass.'

Ned's ice cream was about to fall from the cone and he had no idea. It was making Maz fidgety, she would be needed soon.

'My money's on the priest. I mean he is Creepsville, Arizona — why else would he so promptly deliver this suspiciously empty box? I'd say he scared the nun into delivering the sick children to the room; maybe he was using her as a sex slave as well — yep, wouldn't put it past someone like him, and by that I mean a Catholic cleric. He cleaned the town up, my arse. His arse. Did Veronica say there was a note in a box with 'IOU' written on it? Like an actual physical library for paedo priests with a preference for hard copy. Father Frank shares his collection, he swaps. Fuck me dead: a library of children in underpants. He really should learn how to use a computer. That's it. It was the priest, with a camera, in the sick bay.' She pounced to catch her boy's ice cream but failed.

Ned was now crying so loudly that Luca could not hear the telly and was crying too. Maz scooped up Ned and sat back on the couch.

'Do you miss work?' Fran said.

'Even peak-hour traffic.' She directed Ned's thumb into his mouth and paused to reminisce. 'You have to go to the police. I can come with you.'

Fran put the photos in the hatbox and back in the bag. She didn't want to see those photos ever again. 'There's not enough to go on, and it's ancient news, like the sick bay's been closed forever. No-one's in danger now. Plus I'm on one hell of a learning curve with Dad.'

Wee Ned was bored, and returned to sit in melted ice cream, which didn't seem to worry Maz at all. She found her glass of wine and had a sip.

'You can make that decision if you're the only victim. Otherwise I don't think it's your decision to make. Also, I think maybe it's different if you have little ones still growing up here.'

'Victim?' Fran wanted to swear but the kids were within cooee. She was not a fucking victim, not a fucking gain. 'Vonny was legless — what does dozens mean, even? She's falling in love again and being all dramatic.'

'Rosie wasn't as pissed, right? You could ask her?'

'Should I ask The Captain?'

'The *Captain*! Oh my God.'

'Shut up.' She was already texting him, though, and punctuation decisions were taking an awful long time. This is what she showed Maz for pre-send approval:

Hi there

(She had added and deleted 'Brian' and 'BR' and 'BRJ' and The Captain, before deciding he should be called nothing, in writing at least.)

V says there were 'dozens' of other boxes in the cellar. Wondering if she saw right? Don't want to involve Rosie but wondering if she's said anything to you?

(The question mark at the end was the most difficult decision. She was not of the belief that an x meant anything substantial. However, she decided she should not use one.)

Fran held the phone with both hands and stared hard.

'Fran fancies The Captain!' said Maz.

To prove how little she cared, Fran put the phone down and looked at something else.

'He is the nicest man I've ever met,' said Maz.

'Too nice,' said Fran.

'The words of a thoroughly broken woman. I reckon he'd bring you freshly brewed coffee in bed every morning if you asked,' said Maz. 'You would ask, wouldn't you, not just mope around wishing he did it when he didn't know you wanted him to? You're not a complete idiot are you?'

Fran and Maz were used to having conversations with themselves while in each other's company.

'I don't trust the police here,' said Fran. She was remembering Mr O'Mally, the top cop in the eighties. He *was* the police, and for a short while, she was friends with his little girl, Hilda. They lived in a huge, newly built house near the Gallagher dam, with an enormous garage that had amazing things in it, and Fran had the best days ever playing there. Mr O'Mally collected old games machines, like pinball and ones that had women in them with clothes on. If you got the special coins from the old coin machine, and put one in, the woman's clothes would come off, frame by frame. As a seven-year-old, Fran thought it was disgusting, and couldn't get enough of it. She loved playing there till Hilda suggested they play doctors and nurses. She didn't get that game at all.

There were rumours on the grandstand after the eighties, that Hilda's dad and Father Alfonzo were a team. Fran didn't trust the police.

'*The Captain* makes amazing bread every morning,' said Maz. 'He gave Ciara some when I was at Mum and Dad's for the weekend and she ate the whole loaf, fuming, she said it was amazing. You would totally get home-made bread for brekky. Bet he toasts it perfectly, dark and even, all the way to the edges, bet he makes jam.'

Fran wasn't into jam, especially with bits. She'd eaten too many apricots in her youth. 'They say the town got a good cleansing after the eighties, but it's still a shit magnet. How long have I been here? And everything is still horrible, people tossing ugly crap in my face. I didn't get away all those years at all. It was all still here, waiting for me, festering.'

'Oh for God's sake, what was waiting?'

'Dunno.'

'Depressed Fran alert.'

'My mum got run over by a truck in North Road, my only friend at school dived headfirst off the monument, the Captain's brother shot himself in that paddock over there, and apparently darkness is still lingering on in a wine cellar in yonder convent. You think this place gets over things? I've had too much wine.'

'Jesus, Joseph and Mary, you've had one glass.' Maz refilled it. 'This time I want fun Fran.'

'There's a fun Fran?'

'Allegedly. Tell you what, prove it: holiday Monday, get here any time after ten but before eleven, which is when you and The Captain will begin drinking shots provided by *moi*. He's got a good body considering he's a man.'

'You've seen him? He's got a girly body?'

'No.'

'He has man boobs, hasn't he?'

'No man boobage. I dunno what you call what

125

he's got. What do you want him to have?'

'No beer belly.'

'Tick, esque. He's fifty.'

'Forty-seven. Chest hair.'

'Oh, really?'

'I don't like tiny nipples, but I also don't like those thick, ripe, juicy, inside-of-a-plum-type nipples.'

'You're quite particular re nipples.'

'I'd rather he had none.'

'You're going to kiss him on the lips, Franchy.'

'He won't be able to come Monday. He has a wedding. Dante's dad, in fact. The boarder I 'rooted' when I was a kid. Makes me want to gag. I hope I don't see him. Hope no-one sends me a photo.'

'Oh my God, The Boarder, really? This town *is* a shit magnet.'

'Told you.'

'Okay, The Captain has a wedding. I need a new plan. Why don't you use our pool at night? Any night. I'll leave the lights on. We're dead to the world by eleven and there's a jacuzzi and a wee fire pit. Promise not to peek.'

'That is so creepy. I think you're the one who needs a shag.'

'I can have one, tonight. I might. Probably won't. Maybe I should. Put the effort in, stay awake. Maybe I will. But you need to get out there and hunt for one, in my pool. If I peek I'll feel bad and retract immediately, I probably won't see a thing. You need to get out there Fran, honestly. He'll be nice to cuddle, The Captain — he does give a good hug platonically. And he'll

126

be grateful, you know. That can go a long way, particularly considering your criminally lengthy sexual drought and persistent failure to groom. Imagine — coffee, homemade rye, apricot jam, The Captain's bringing it all to you in bed. He's dressed in his — what do you want him to be in?'

'Chinos.'

'At breakfast time?'

'Yep.'

'He's in his chinos at eight-thirty in the morning . . . nup, I'm out. What a waste of a fantasy . . . He's only ever had his wife, you know. No-one since then that I've heard of, though many have tried, including Tricia Gallagher's sister Beth — God she hates your guts.'

The second glass over, Maz put it down and slapped her thighs. That was as far as she would go. Maz was an expert at getting drunk for ten minutes before returning fully focused to the job at hand. They made their way to the door. 'This town's no more shit than any other place,' she said. 'It's just that when you live in a small town, you know everyone, you know their tragedies, and you feel their pain. If you don't like it here then fuck off, or stop hating it. We tried to fuck off, no luck, now we're not hating it. It's not so hard.'

Maz had left the door open too long, and Ned had escaped. He was halfway up the drive already. Luca stood beside his mother, watching his little brother with a grin. He was gonna get in so much trouble.

'If you catch him and bring him back I'll give you a Choo Choo Bar,' Maz said to her seven-year-old.

Luca sprinted off almost immediately — his reactions were a little slow — and he was getting tired already. He may not reach his little brother, who was almost at the end of the driveway.

'Hurry Luca!' Maz yelled. 'He's always trying to get to Bri's . . . The Captain's. Have you seen their rescue pups? It's all too cute.'

Luca had tackled Ned and they had landed on the gravel. They were crying.

'Gimme your Choo Choo Bar,' Maz said.

Fran realised she was referring to the one in her treasure box. 'That one? It's thirty years old!'

Maz's stare was serious, so Fran retrieved the liquorice treat from her hatbox and handed it over.

Luca grabbed the lolly and began trying to open it, but the wrapper was cemented to the insides. 'How do you get this open? Haha, look what I've got! How do you? Mum?'

'Don't worry, I'm not gonna let him eat it,' Maz said, kissing her friend goodbye. 'Chin up, Franch. As someone once said on the internet: Make the most of the bad times cos the catastrophic times are just around the corner.'

20

The Day of the Fire

MAZ

Maz is emptying ice into a bowl from her whizz-bang freezer. It's dark in the house: the blinds and the shutters are closed. Her boys, Ned and Luca, are lying on the wooden living room floor in front of *Thomas the Tank Engine*.

This is the most successful open house since they arrived — several families have come and gone, cooling themselves in the pool, relaxing in front of the aircon (which was working till 2.00 pm). The last arrivals, now too hot to move, are Tricia Gallagher, her cousin/husband Chook, and their grandchildren: Bradley, six; Kinsey, four; and Brianna, one, who's in a nappy and asleep on her playmat. Everyone else is awake and in bathers. The four over-threes are wet from jumping in the shower. Bowls of ice have been placed around the room, with fans blowing over them. The humans are struggling. It's forty-five outside and thirty-two in.

Tricia's twenty-six-year-old daughter, Emily, has been texting incessantly, and there's no sign of her letting up. It's the first time Tricia and Chook have looked after all three grandchildren overnight.

Stop worrying! the young granny messages.

Waiting for cool change then heading home.

'Can we get in the pool again?' says Ned.

'Soon as the change comes,' says Ciara.

'Gotta be soon,' says Tricia.

'It's freezing in Adelaide,' says Chook.

'Twenty-three,' says Tricia. 'Is that a breeze?'

'No,' says Chook.

'Is that thunder?' says Tricia.

'Nah,' says Chook.

'All the flavour's gone!' Luca's referring to his frozen bottle of organic raspberry cordial — well it was once raspberry, now it's a small block of smooth, unsuckable, ungettable ice — which he is using as a very loud musical instrument.

'Come, I'll add some of this,' Maz yells from the kitchen area.

Luca heads to the kitchen. Ned, Brady and Kinsey follow, each holding up their flavourless frozen bottles, into which Maz pours home-made lemon cordial.

In the lounge, Tricia says to Chook: 'What's that noise?' She no longer trusts her senses.

In the kitchen, Maz says to Ciara: 'That's the town siren.'

'You sure?' Ciara asks.

Maz is sure.

'Holy shit,' Ciara whispers.

'I'll get rid of them.' Maz enters the living room and claps. 'That's the town siren everyone. No updates online yet but best be safe. Up, up, adventure time, oval time. You and Chook good to get there in your car, Trish?'

'You sure it's the emergency siren?' asks Trish. She tells Trish she is sure, and that it's an extended siren, which is scarier than a short one, but even Maz is a doubting Thomas. She presses the shutter button and the northern blinds ascend very slowly; at first all she and the others can see is the edge of the swimming pool, then some of the blue — green water before the blinds crunch and stop. Maz presses the button again.

Everyone's head is pointing down; going slowly up. The Perspex fence comes into view; then some dead grass on the other side of the pool. The shutter is also too hot to move and crunches upwards, millimetre by millimetre.

There is more yellow grass . . .

There will be sky in a moment, blue probably, white or grey hopefully. Please let there be clouds — Maz, like everyone, is making a wish, and expecting the worst news will be blue.

The sky isn't blue. It's black and it's red and it's grey. Not sky but fire. The sky is on fire. And it is coming straight for the house.

Maz presses the button over and over, and the shutter begins to descend.

Trish and Chook are already gathering their grandchildren.

'We'll follow you,' Trish says, about to exit the front door.

'Um, no you go first,' says Ciara. 'We'll be a few minutes. Got to get a few things.'

'Forget about fuckin' things!' says Tricia's husband, Chook.

'Don't swear,' says Tricia.

'There's a fucking fire!' Chook rushes out to the car. He puts Brianna in the car seat in the back; and buckles Brady and Kinsey in either side.

'I want to go on the oval adventure!' Ned is saying.

'I want to go with Brady and Kinsey!' Luca is saying.

'I want to go in the pool,' Kinsey sobs from the backseat. 'You promised. I don't want the oval.'

All five children are now howling.

Maz picks up Ned and Ciara scoops up Luca. Nothing will separate them from the boys.

'Get in the car,' Chook says to Trish, who is still waiting at the door for her friends to exit, but they are not taking action.

'We're not leaving without you. Hurry, please,' Trish says.

'Trish, listen — I have to tell you . . . '

Maz has stopped Ciara from finishing the sentence and dragged her and the boys into the laundry. She shuts the door, puts earphones on Luca's head and her hands over Ned's ears. 'Don't you dare. We've discussed this.'

'But Kinsey and Brianna! Me for those two, please, I'll make sure to be safe.'

'I promised to stop you if this happened, and you promised to stop me,' Maz says, shutting Ciara and the boys in the laundry, and wedging the door behind her.

Maz heads out to make sure Tricia et al leave. 'We'll follow in two secs,' she says.

Behind her, Ciara is banging on the laundry window and is trying to write something on the dusty glass with her finger.

'Don't be crazy and get in the bunker,' Trish says.

'Bunker?' Maz is bad at lying.

'The one you built before moving in.'

'Everyone knows about your bunker,' Chook says, revving the engine, desperate to leave. 'They're death traps those things, please come with us.'

'It's accredited,' Maz finds herself saying.

'Well, good luck.' Chook gives her a sad look, as if he will never see her again, then takes off down the drive, a cloud of dust following his hatchback towards the safety of the town oval.

PART THREE

THE VESTRY

21

Six Days before the Fire

'You should never have given me your digits,' Fran said. She'd had too much wine with Maz.

'Sorry?' The Captain was distracted. Several children were squawking in the background and someone was either playing the drums or shooting people.

'My timing's off. I'll call tomorrow.'

'Fran! No, no,' he said, adding another three no's as he removed himself from the noise. Fran heard a door close. He took a breath. 'Sorry — bath time! Want some children?'

'Um . . . '

'Rosie had one photo, but it didn't show anything, I was about to get back to you.'

'So you can't see more boxes?'

'Can't see any.'

'That's good.'

'It is.'

A horse neighed in the paddock to Fran's left.

'Where are you?' said The Captain.

'Walking home from Maz's.'

'South two?'

'Yeah.'

'Can you do me a favour, check the gate's padlocked? Oh, and the little girls keep asking when you're gonna visit.'

Fran had reached the gate to the Ryan's South

2 paddock, just one removed from the ostrich enclosure. 'I forgot! The cheese.' She could take it to his place tomorrow — no, that would be too eager. 'So the gate's closed, but the padlock's not locked, the chain's on the ground.'

'You're joking.'

'No.'

'I locked it an hour ago, wrapped the chain securely. I lock it every evening. For the last month, someone has been unlocking it.'

'Who?'

'Rosie's been staking it out, says she's seen her Uncle Martin.'

'But,' Fran had the chain in her hand. The paddock was still and silent — 'Martin is dead.'

'BOO!!'

The Captain had yelled so loudly that she dropped the phone. 'Arsehole.' She picked it up.

'Are you free at all on Saturday? Forecast says it's gonna be a scorcher and our groom developed second thoughts at his stag do in Bali. Do you want to hang out at the college pool? That's where I'm gonna be with the kids — take a picnic?'

The college pool. Fran had vowed never to go there again. 'If I can get the nurse, I'd love to,' she said.

'I've got three weddings between now and then. I'm starting to agree with you and Vonny.'

'What?'

'Weddings are sadder than funerals.'

'What are you talking about? You had a happy marriage.'

'She died!'

They both laughed.

'See ya in the deep end, Francesca Collins.'

★ ★ ★

Fran could see the disco lights from the end of the driveway. Dante had set them up in the living room. Linda Rondstadt's 'Blue Bayou' was blaring. Dante and Gramps were stoned, sitting opposite each other, making very odd faces, and giggling like crazy.

'Sit here, we're finger and face dancing!' Dante said.

Dante always had such fabulous ideas. 'But you've got the wrong song.' Fran changed the record to Daddy Cool's 'Eagle Rock' and took a chair in the triangle. All three of them were very competitive. Dante had excellent movable eyebrows, Fran used her tongue and nostrils with great creativity and could do a mean 'Eagle Rock' with her finger and thumb. But it was Gramps who pulled out the winning move — at the climax too, he had built it well. Without touching, he wriggled his left ear in time with the music — *I'm just crazy 'bout the way you move* — then his left ear joined in — *Doin' the Eagle Rock.*

The three of them were sore from laughing when the song ended.

22

Three Days before the Fire

The routines were less depressing already. Fran's goals were small, time was plentiful, her patient very lovable. She no longer missed people-packed streets, wearing shoes she couldn't run in and staring at a screen all day in the job she'd accidentally had for many years. Most of all, she didn't miss being with a man who didn't love her enough, and who she didn't love enough either. She was starting to wonder why she'd been so reluctant to leave it all behind.

It was only lunchtime, but it was already well over thirty-five degrees. The air-conditioning in her dad's four-wheel drive didn't have time to take effect by the time she reached The Captain's. Camembert was leaking out of its bag onto the passenger seat. She rescued what she could, and knocked on the door.

There was no-one in the farmhouse. Fran walked round the side and along the track towards the old shearing shed. She'd never ventured into the heart of the Ryan farm. It was a mysterious wonderland that she knew nothing about. She loved it.

The nine-year-old twins were playing Jacks in the old dipping trenches.

'Hey girdles, I have something for you.' Fran had bought the cheese at Annie Gray's farm

140

shop. She sat beside the country ragamuffins, both dressed only in large T-shirts, which Fran realised probably belonged to their late mother. 'Now I know one of you is called Amy,' she said, opening the greaseproof paper to reveal the beauties she had purchased — a huge slab of Roquefort and a very runny Camembert.

'I'm Harriet,' said the other one, whose T-shirt was pink.

Amy, closest to the cheese, and in a blue T-shirt, looked on with disgust as the Camembert oozed out onto the paper. 'It smells like vomit.'

Excellent. Having given it some thought, Fran didn't feel at all comfortable smuggling the girls food that wrecked the planet, considering their dad was trying so hard to save it. Also, she wanted the cheeses. She'd bought a nice Malbec and some peppery crackers to have with them. 'If you think that one's strong, you should taste the blue, it's got mould in it,' she said.

The girls looked depressed. 'That's disgusting!'

'Yuk!'

Fran was about to wrap it up again when Harriet leaned over and dipped her finger in the dripping Camembert. Her shaky finger made its way to her mouth, the dollop entering tentatively, her eyes closing as she took in the texture and flavour of the cheese, then opening wide in anger and horror: 'Has this existed all my life?'

Amy, realising the cheese was obviously good, plunged her finger into it and had a taste. Both of them were so overwhelmed they were on the verge of tears.

'Quick,' said Amy, looking round. 'We need to get this out of here.' And the girls raced off to hide the cheese.

★ ★ ★

Fran knew she looked keen coming here today. To hell with it, she was.

The old shearing shed was as rustic as the cheese. The Captain was out, according to his chef — a Syrian named Sami. He and Perla lived in the old shearing quarters and did most of the wedding graft.

'No worries,' said Fran. 'Who you got today, then?'

Sami checked his tablet. 'Mr and Mrs Jones from Benalla, renewing their vows after ten years, no difficult allergies, nothing to indicate they're dicks.'

'I give them a year,' said Fran.

The space was already beautiful. There were hay bales at both ends of the open wooden shed. Candles in jars lined the inner rafters, the tables were made of old sleepers, and the chairs were all different shapes and sizes. There were potted flowers and herbs everywhere — Perla was arranging them on the tables at the other end of the shed. The guests would look out from their tables at horses grazing in the paddock yonder, and many other farm delights: chooks and puppies and goats and pigs and lambs and flowers and fruit and veg and tractors, and farmers. Fran would get married here in a heartbeat if she was the marrying type.

She found herself leaving as fast as she could. The Captain might get home and read her thoughts.

★ ★ ★

Dante arrived at seven with Nonna's fusilli pomarola, a beetroot and red onion tarte Tatin, and a girlfriend called Tiffany whose neck was one sprawling, blue, floral tattoo.

'So nice to meet you,' said Tiffany.

'Hi, Tiffany.' Dante hadn't mentioned the woman. Ever since Lucia broke his heart in Viareggio, he'd had a two-date rule. And Fran had never even met Lucia.

'I love your name — *Francesca*,' said Tiffany, 'especially the -chesca part. Can I call you *Chesca*?'

She wanted to say no, not Chesca, certainly not to you. 'Call me whatever you want,' she said, wondering what she was supposed to talk to this Tiffany about and deciding on food: 'You hungry?' She'd forgotten to tell Dante that the two V's were bringing Japanese takeaway for dinner.

An hour later, the table was crammed with an odd assortment of hot and cold foods, and an even odder assortment of people: disabled father, disgruntled daughter, ex-something-or-other, clever son and his stupid girlfriend.

She was finding it difficult to look at Vincent. When she did, her heart sank. He was on call at

143

the housing association all weekend, so she'd see him off quick smart after the meal.

'I have good news,' said Dante, taking Tiffany's heavily manicured hand.

'Don't waste good news on me,' said Gramps, who'd been nodding on and off for half an hour.

'Tiffany and I are officially boyfriend and girlfriend.' He kissed her on the lips.

Everyone looked away.

'That's such good news,' said Fran. Dante had obviously been watching too much *Love House*, or was stuck in the eighties, when boys passed notes to girls saying: *Will you go with me?*

'To celebrate we're heading to the beach for a few days. Wondering if we could take the four-wheel drive? My car's in the garage.'

Obviously, Tiffany didn't have a vehicle of her own. Or a purpose. 'Sure,' Fran said. She didn't need a car. Gramps was still refusing to leave the house, and she preferred walking or running anyway.

Vonny had been texting since she arrived, the beep going off incessantly, no-one daring to ask her to mute it. Each time she read a message, a little smile appeared on her face that she probably thought was secret. It was making Fran angry. Her own mobile was in her pocket and her thigh had not vibrated once. 'Can you at least turn off the beep?' Fran said at last.

Vonny put her phone on silent. 'Can I be excused?'

'Sure,' said Vincent.

They'd not finished the meal, and Vincent knew it was a family rule to stay until everyone

144

was done. Fran was angry enough to almost look him in the eye.

'Can I go to Rosie's?' said Vonny.

'Sure,' said Fran.

Vincent was mad now. He didn't know this Rosie girl, or her family.

'Ring and I'll collect you,' Fran said, excited that she might see The Captain tonight. A moment later, when her mobile vibrated in her pocket, she jumped in her chair with excitement. As hoped, it was The Captain:

Thanks for the cheese! Amy is doing the smelliest farts. DO NOT LIGHT A MATCH!

OMG sorry, she replied, *my plan failed. Sitting here with Dante's new gf. I am the mother-in-law!*

Excellent, you can be a rude bitch. Mother-in-laws are allowed, it's the perk.

Already coming naturally . . . 40 tomorrow.

I know. We'll be at the pool at 12, staying all day. Bring some shade with you x

He'd put an x!

Will do, Fran typed, smiling to herself the way Vonny just had, then adding an x of her own.

When she finally looked up, she accidentally caught Vincent in the eye, but her mood was so high that he only made a dent in it.

'I'll see you to the door,' she said.

Fran and Vincent's bad moods never lasted more than an hour or so, during which time they tended to remain silent and avoid each other, which was what they were doing now.

'We'll never get enough time together to get over tiffs,' she said.

'What are you talking about?'

'You can't be my best friend anymore. Constance won't allow it.'

'Sure she will.'

'No she won't. No woman would. I wouldn't.'

'You're being daft.' Vincent hugged her. 'I love you. I'll always be here for you.'

He left for Melbourne a minute later.

★   ★   ★

She waved Dante and Tiffany off in the four-wheel drive at 9.30 pm, then remembered she'd offered to collect Vonny. Bugger. She was about to text when she walked in the door with Rosie. 'Do you mind if we have a sleepover tonight?' Vonny asked.

'Dad's learning the flute,' Rosie explained.

Fran watched as they headed to her old bedroom and closed the door. She wondered what the rules should be, and whether she should check with The Captain. She'd let Dante's girlfriend sleep over at sixteen (after he promised to use protection). Decision made — intervening would be discriminatory. Anyway, they might just be friends. She hoped so, for selfish reasons. She was not keen on an incestuous *Brady Bunch* situation.

23

Two Days before the Fire

No Spitting, No Swearing, No Running, No Diving, No Bombing.

The sign had been at the deep end for as long as Fran could remember. With so many petty rules to spoil the fun, no wonder more serious offences had happened here.

She'd taken her time loading the wheelbarrow — several items were packed into the makeshift ice bucket on wheels and then retrieved. The bottle of Prosecco, for example, which she decided would appear very flirty on ice, and so hid in her food backpack to consider later. In the end, the wheelbarrow was a work of genius organisation. She'd wheeled it down the driveway, right along Ryan's Lane, then skirted the fence separating the ostriches and South 1. She was boiling when she reached the playing fields, and thankful that the college and its surrounds appeared to be abandoned.

The no-frills seventies rectangle was mostly surrounded by concrete. Fran parked her barrow under the only trees at the western end, and began unloading onto the small grass area. Her T-shirt was dripping with sweat. She peeled her clothes off and jumped into the pool. Ah, the relief, already, and it was only noon.

Sari and Speedo dripping, Fran erected three

sun tents and two umbrellas. She placed two armchairs in the area most likely to receive afternoon shade and was about to jump in the pool again when Amy and Harriet raced in.

'You poisoned us!' said Amy.

'She shat her pants,' said Harriet.

'I did not,' said Amy.

'Did so,' said Harriet.

'Did not!' Amy looked like she might break one or more of the pool rules.

Her dad arrived just in time. 'First in wins!'

The twins jumped in.

(Fran would have checked what the prize was first.)

Thirteen-year-old Cathy, who was carrying a cabin-sized suitcase on wheels, walked purposefully to one of Fran's tents, and zipped herself and her luggage inside.

'Oi, that's not yours, Cathy,' said The Captain, whose load rivalled Fran's. 'This place is gonna look like Woodstock,' he said. He had four sun tents — and (despite Fran's protestations that she could stay put) installed Cathy into one of them. He also had three umbrellas, two loungers, two Eskies, and a dinky set of speakers. 'What do you want to feel? Happy, sad, excited?'

It took her a moment to realise he was referring to song choice. Her instinct was to say 'excited', but that'd be up there with Prosecco on ice. Also, she was already excited, and could probably do with bringing it down a notch. 'Gentle at first? We can build up to the ACDC.' Damn, that was way worse than 'excited'.

The Captain chose to shuffle his country-and-western playlist, and the first song was as gentle as can be. Even so, Fran was getting more keyed up by the second.

A moment later, they did bombs in the deep end. He swam underwater to scare his ragamuffin twins, hurling them in the air one at a time, then swam up to Fran, who was in the shallow end: 'Would you like some tea ma'am?'

'Do you have any Earl Grey?' she said, diving down and joining him cross-legged on the floor of the pool, raising her little finger to take a sip.

The next hour was idyllic. Cathy exited her tent with earplugs and swim cap and did at least a hundred lengths, Aussie crawl, then zipped herself back in to read. The twins splashed about in their full-body swimwear, wet hats covering neck and ears, popping out for more sun cream and a sip from one of Fran's frozen bottles, which were a hit — yay. By 1.00 pm, Fran felt confident enough to choose songs that made her excited, and to put the Prosecco in the barrow among the icy bottles.

Then Vonny and Rosie arrived. They'd been down the street, hangin' around. Neither was willing to waste time offering more information than that. They picked up a tent and an umbrella and set up camp on the grass as far away as possible.

'Take it your dad didn't want to come?' said The Captain.

'Said he'd rather be paralysed. It'd be a bit dodgy, too, don't you think — an old man's head on a stick watching over the kiddies in the yellow end?'

Vonny and Rosie were now zipped inside their tent, laughing.

'Listen, I let them stay in the same room last night. Are you okay with that?'

'I think so,' he said.

'I think so, too.'

'They might just be friends,' he said.

Vonny and Rosie had stopped laughing. Their tent had gone silent.

'Zippers open everyone!' Fran yelled.

'Zippers open NOW!' The Captain clapped.

'Jeez,' Vonny said as she unzipped. The girls had an earphone in each, and were listening to something on Rosie's iPhone. They unplugged and moved their camp onto the concrete at the very edge of the deep end. With the mouth of the tent open, they dangled their feet in the pool, a true crime podcast playing quietly from the iPhone.

The zipper incident changed the mood, and it took a further turn when two boarders arrived, neither of whom Fran had seen around town. Boarder #6 dived straight in the shallow end, nothing with him to shed before doing so. Boarder #7, weedier than his friend, followed suit. They had a tennis ball, which they tossed to each other, eyeing the tent at the other end of the pool every so often. There were two girls up there around the same age as them.

'Can you see what's happening?' Fran said. She and The Captain were lying on their tummies under the shade of an umbrella, their faces to the pool, life-guarding.

Boarder #6 threw the ball to Boarder #7.

'Yeah, they're zig-zagging, gradually moving towards the other end . . . I can't tell you how happy I am Rosie's not into boys.'

'Tell me about it,' said Fran.

The boys' throws were becoming more obvious. They would soon need to tread water.

The mouth of the girls' tent seemed ominous, especially with four feet coming out of it, ten toes dipping the water.

'It's like we're watching Jaws,' said Fran.

The boys were splashing, moving closer to the gaping mouth at the end of the pool.

'Duunnn dunn . . . ' said The Captain.

'But who's the shark? The girls or the boys?'

The boys were now treading water and finding it more difficult to throw and catch the tennis ball. They were flailing a tad, splashing, vulnerable, just tiny bobbing heads. Yet somehow, they were still managing to move in the right direction.

The Captain rolled onto his side and faced Fran. Intimate, sudden, like what he then said: 'So Maz suggested we should use her pool.'

Oh Lord. *Maz.*

'It's going to be impossible to sleep tomorrow night. I was thinking . . . '

'Look, look,' she said. The boys were nearly at the very end. Soon they would lean their elbows on the edge of the pool and ask the girls a question. For instance: *G'day, want a root?*

He touched her arm to get her attention. 'So it's so hot tomorrow night, maybe we could do

151

that, go to the pub, then have a swim at Maz's.'

'Just you and me?' she said. His hand was still on her arm. 'Under the stars, a little intoxicated, having a swim?'

A definite beat.

'I need to get in the pool!' he said, running off and diving in.

She sat up and smiled. The power! Then she heard Boarder #7.

'Hey girls,' he said to Vonny and Rosie. 'What are you doing in there?'

Fran ran over and bombed the boarders, almost skimming #7's shoulder. Her splash was impressive, certainly scared them off.

★　★　★

The afternoon heat took care of the bad energy. The two lethargic boarders came and went, last time with some beers they did not try to hide. The kids jumped in and out of the pool to cool themselves. They ate sandwiches, drank cordial (no longer frozen) and slept in their tents.

Meanwhile, Fran and her new lover boy drank Prosecco and checked over each other's bodies without even trying to hide it.

'You don't have man boobs,' she said.

'You don't either,' he said.

At around 4.30 pm, Boarders #7 and #8 returned for the fourth time, bringing #1, #2 and #3, last spotted at the monument, with them. The gang staked their claim beside the girls' tent, drinking tinnies on the concrete at the deep end.

152

'We should go,' said Fran.

'Why should we?' said The Captain. 'I'm not moving in this heat.'

Fran kept a very close eye for the next hour. The boys didn't seem to be trying to interact. Thank God. She was about to close her eyes for a snooze when they started shouting and laughing. All five of them had jumped in the pool, and were treading water as they looked into the girls' tent.

Fran dived in to see what they were laughing at — the girls were kissing passionately. Jesus Christ, why was her daughter such a shit-stirrer? The Captain had seen the girls too and when Fran got out of the pool, he shrugged.

Apart from everything else, their daughters were more than friends, which meant the parents could never be.

The boarders were getting rowdy. Three of them were out of the pool now, poking at the fabric of the tent. Their comments floated round the rectangle like the ghosts of bigots past: 'Lezzies! Can I come in for a threesome?' 'I'll turn you if you give me a shot.' 'Hey, Mountain Dykes, let us in!'

Vonny and Rosie managed to get out of the tent and race across to the family camp.

'What dickheads,' Vonny said.

'Why did you provoke them?' said Fran.

'How did we provoke them?' said Vonny.

She was right. Was she right?

'I'll get your things, move you back here,' said The Captain.

'No, no way,' said Rosie. 'We'll get our own things.'

She and Vonny, obviously firmly attached at the hip forevermore, stormed off hand in hand to gather their tent and belongings, neither of them remotely intimidated by the boarders, the third of whom greeted Rosie with:

'I reckon you could do better than her.'

Rosie ignored him, tried to grab her towel, but Boarder #3 was standing on it. She pulled harder, and won. The tent wasn't so easy. Both girls were pulling at it, but at least three boys were holding it back. They were one-trick arseholes.

'Let go dickwads,' said Rosie.

'Aw c'mon, no need to get nasty, we just want to play. Stay,' said Boarder #6.

Making the most of a lapse in attention, the girls yanked the tent and walked away with their belongings.

'The redhead's basic anyway,' said Boarder #1.

'The other one's a truck,' said Boarder #7.

'Aw, don't be mean,' said Boarder #3, 'she's not bad looking for an Abo.'

Vonny and Rosie froze, their tent between them.

Keep walking Vonny, Fran was thinking. *Remember what your dad always tells you and not what your mum always tells you.*

It was Rosie, actually, who turned around and said: 'What did you say?' She then walked up to Boarder #3 and said it again. 'What did you say?'

Rosie and Boarder #3 were nose to nose. Everyone else froze.

'I said,' said Boarder #3, edging a millimetre

154

closer, 'she's not bad looking for an Abo.'

Fran wasn't fast enough, nor was Vonny, nor was The Captain. Rosie had punched Boarder #3 so hard that he stumbled backwards into the pool and disappeared into the body of the deep end.

Fran raced over to the girls. 'Are you all right?'

Boarder #3 bobbed up out of the water, his nose bleeding. 'Are *they* all right?'

The other boarders were already fleeing the scene.

Boarder #3's lip may have quivered a little when he noticed his friends had abandoned him. He left a pink trail as he side-stroked to the middle of the pool, then water-walked all the way to the ladder at the other end, sobbing as he staggered out the pool gate, leaving drops of nose blood in his wake.

⋆　⋆　⋆

They packed their things quickly.

The Captain's mood had turned. 'Hurry,' he kept saying to his girls.

They were about to part ways at the gate when Father Frank marched towards them, five towelled boarders in tow.

'I hear there's been an incident.' Father Frank stopped two metres before reaching them, his flock behind him, theirs behind them.

'She punched me,' said Boarder #3, pointing at Rosie.

Father Frank looked at Rosie, who was hiding behind her dad, and seemed to have shrunk.

155

'What kind of *wuss* are you, Bagshaw?' said the priest to Boarder #3.

'But they were kissing, her and her, in the tent.'

Father Frank turned his head slowly. He needed to hear this again. 'What was that?'

'Those two, they were winding us up, putting on a show, tongue kissing in the tent. They're lesbians.'

Father Frank paused before delivering his decision: 'I won't call the police about the assault if you leave immediately, all of you. We do not approve of that kind of behaviour here.'

'You mean kissing? What's the big deal?' Rosie said.

Father Frank could barely contain his rage: 'It's a big deal to God, a very big deal.'

'That's ridiculous,' Fran said. 'Don't listen to a word he's saying, girls.'

'Did you not hear me?' said Father Frank. 'Leave immediately. And if I ever see one of you on this property without permission again, I will make that call to the police.'

The families parted in silence — the Ryans heading to their car out front, the Collins womenfolk and their wheelbarrow towards the playing fields.

'Oi,' Father Frank yelled when they had almost reached the grandstand. 'Where do you think you're going? You're trespassing on college property. You go the other way, using the exit.'

When Fran and Vonny reached the carpark, the Ryans had disappeared, and they had to wheel that wheelbarrow all the way home. At the convent, Fran spotted the nun staring at her from a window. She was dressed in her full habit, as ever. It was forty-one degrees.

'That woman must stink,' said Vonny.

She was still staring. Awkward. Fran waved, and the nun nodded back.

'She is creepy as all fuck,' said Vonny.

24

The Day of the Fire

SISTER MARY MARGARET

Sister Mary Margaret was Eliza Winterton once upon a time, and had decided to be her again today. She was even wearing the sixties floral maxi she'd last worn for her graduation.

Her habit was in the fireplace. She had built a pretty stick pyramid and placed it on top. She'd get off the sofa and light it shortly, but this was a solemn ritual, there was no hurry.

When she first put the habit on, she remembered she felt safe for the first time in her life. She believed it was a magic cloak. She soon discovered that the habit didn't make her invisible to predators, it made her an accessory.

Never again.

She was drenched in sweat from the heat already, and yet staggered over to the hearth and lit the fire. She watched as the paper and kindling took off, and smiled as it began to lick at her old uniform.

She lit a cigarette, inhaled, and held it loosely. She saluted the Housewives of New York and skulled her pink drink in one, immediately pouring another and doing the same. She had been celebrating for two hours, and would continue to do so until she was unconscious.

She tossed a set of beads into the fire and was certain they hissed. She didn't need them. She knew heaven was off the table.

She settled into the couch. 'Hi,' she said to the girls on the telly. 'My name might be Izzy, but I sure ain't dizzy.'

She had seen the priest off two hours ago, then locked the gate and thrown the key in with the general waste. No dark vehicles would crunch her gravel again. There was no reason, now the cellar was empty. Now the children were gone.

The habit was dust, the fire weakening, her eyes closing. At last, unconsciousness was coming. She hugged her empty glass to her chest. Her cigarette fell into the overflowing ashtray on the floor beneath her. Such a quiet thing, the coming of unconsciousness.

Were her eyes open? She thought they were closed but everything was bright red. She tested it out — open, shut, open — shut, and decided she must be asleep. She often saw hell in her sleep, after all. And when the noise came, Sister Mary Margaret didn't question it. She often heard hell in her sleep too, and it was often as loud as this.

25

One Day before the Fire

Fran wasn't the only one to choose the 8.30 am. It was going to be hot again, maybe even hotter than yesterday, if you could imagine. St Michael's was jampacked with people wearing their lightest Sunday clothes and fanning their faces with hymn books. She'd been in and out of the cold shower all night, had even spent a few hours on the veranda, but there were too many hazards out there: the wind had picked up and was hot and dusty and thick. The mozzies were hungry, buzzing around the outside light. They would eat her alive and so would a snake, probably, or a spider. There were spiders in every corner, many of them with the potential to kill her while she lay sleeping. A bull had appeared on the veranda once, when she was ten. It wasn't safe out there, and it wasn't any cooler than inside anyway. It wasn't just the heat that had kept her awake. It was like she'd been dropped without even getting the note saying, *Will you go with me?*

She totally would have. But his daughter had been in trouble twice since meeting hers.

And vice versa. Fuck's sake. Vonny hadn't punched anyone. That was his kid. Screw him if he was being judgemental.

Father Frank never usually did the early mass

and Fran would have walked out again if it hadn't taken her two hours to persuade Gramps (on a stick) to come. She was in a seat at the back, her dad's head beside her in the aisle. They could hardly hear Father Frank's sermon.

'What did he say?' Gramps bellowed at one point.

This week, Fran was not inclined to turn down the volume. Let him talk. 'Something about footy,' Fran said, also loudly.

'What did he say?' Gramps yelled a moment later. 'What are we supposed to do regarding hand balls?'

'He's making no sense at all,' Fran almost yelled. She recognised many of the faces that turned to give her a dirty look: Sister Mary Margaret, Tricia Gallagher and her cousin-lover Chook, and thirteen-year-old Cathy Ryan.

When the collection came, she found herself taking a dollar from the plate and putting it in her pocket.

She deserved a refund.

★   ★   ★

After mass, her dad was determined to go to confession. Bugger.

'Can we not go to The Tree instead?' Fran said. She'd been trying to take him there all week, but he was not having it.

'I have made all the plans I am ever going to make,' he said.

Confession it was. She wheeled him to the waiting area, and sat beside him on a wooden chair, both staring at the solemn curtained booth, which was currently occupied.

Mrs Verity O'Leary came out at last, almost tripping as she did. 'Ah hello!' she said, going bright red. Her sins must have been doozies.

Fran parked Gramps on a Stick in the box and closed the door. 'Can you please yell when you're done, Father?'

'Sure thing,' said Father Frank from inside.

Twenty-five minutes later, Fran was still sitting there. Ridiculous. Her dad hadn't committed one single sin. She knocked on the door: 'Is everything all right?'

'Yes, done,' Father Frank said, coming out of the goody's side and opening the other door.

In the opposite booth, her dad was crying. 'Gonna switch off, Franny,' he said.

She did so immediately.

'He gets down. It's understandable.' Father Frank leaned in: 'By the way, didn't I tell you not to step foot on parish property?'

'Did you mean the church? Can you do that? But what about Dad?'

'I'll drive him here myself, in the flesh, not with that ridiculous contraption of yours.' A group of parishioners were heading their way. Father Frank put his nice voice on. 'I take it you weren't wanting confession, Francesca?'

Suddenly, she did. 'I do, Father. I do.'

★   ★   ★

'Bless me Father for I have sinned,' she said. 'It has been — it's been twenty-nine years and eleven months since my last confession, and these are my sins.'

She was expecting to list numerous venial sins, for example that she had sworn at her daughter three times in the last week and twice fantasised about her father's peaceful death. She had expected to then say: 'For these and all the sins that I have committed during my life, I am deeply sorry.' Instead, this: 'Actually, Father, I can't think of any sins.'

'Take your time, my daughter. We are all sinners.'

Fran took her time. She sat in the dark a long while, then answered, 'Nup.'

'Have you had bad thoughts, perhaps you've disobeyed orders?'

'Anything I tell you, anything at all, you won't tell anyone else?'

'Yes.'

'I have had bad thoughts, I have. About a man.'

'Yes?'

'In a dress.'

'Yes . . . '

'I've fantasised about calling him names: hypocrite, homophobe, pervert. During mass I imagined bludgeoning his head with a baseball bat.'

She waited, but the priest did not respond. In fact, she couldn't even hear him breathe.

'So that's definitely in the bad thoughts category — thought I should mention it. Oh, and I stole a dollar from the collection plate,' she said, slamming the tiny door behind her.

26

One Day before the Fire

Fran had no intention of going to The Red Lion, but Vonny (on her big brother's strict instructions) booted her out at 8.50 pm. She was not to return for at least three hours; she was to get a life.

Thanks, Vonny. She walked along Ryan's Lane in the darkness. She hadn't bothered to change out of her shorts and T-shirt as proof to herself, or as insurance, that she would not wind up at the pub. At the population sign, she felt a vibration on her upper thigh, and took her phone out of her pocket. Nothing. The Captain had not been in touch since the pool incident. Her thigh had developed a psychosomatic alert sensation.

Her shorts and T-shirt were wet with sweat by the time she reached the monument. The eucalyptus forest was still, no leaves shuffling. She was hoping to climb to the top, but the door wouldn't budge. She heard a boy talking on the other side, and a girl laughing.

Fran had at least two and three-quarter hours to fill. She ran down the eastern side of the hill and stopped at the oval, taking in the clear sky at the graffitied feet of Bert Gallagher (two dicks, one on each foot, original).

The tap beside the statue was a tease — no water came out — so she decided to head to the pub for a drink of water, that was all. She was thirsty.

He wouldn't be there anyway. He wouldn't be there waiting for her.

She was right. The Captain wasn't in the bar. Only three people were, all members of the fete committee. They'd moved tomorrow's extravaganza indoors due to the forecast, and were now calling round, gathering as many fans as the mains in the convent would allow.

Tricia Gallagher was waiting on her Bacardi and Coke at the opposite side of the bar. 'I hear your grandfather's statue's about to go,' she said to barman Pete.

'About time,' said Pete, 'he was an aggro fucker.'

'There's quite a strong case for Father Frank,' Tricia said, 'for what he did — rebuilding the town after, well, you know, the difficulties.'

Fran suddenly realised that everything Tricia Kelly had ever said or done irritated her. It wasn't just that Tricia dumped and bullied her when she got pregnant, or that she got with The Boarder for a while. Or that she dropped her all over again when the baby thing got boring — three months after he was born, it was. She and her mean-girl cronies had been round daily after the birth, excited and friendly all of a sudden. They brought gifts, took turns holding Dante, argued over who would push the buggy down North Road. Then Dante started crying a lot. Too much, and Tricia and her friends stopped coming.

Fran often thanked Dante for screaming his

165

lungs out and driving them away. She was happier being a mum on her own. She was really busy.

Tricia's roots were showing, you could see that a mile away. And she was far too skinny for a woman of forty-five. Fran shook herself. She should not waste energy on Tricia Gallagher. The dislike was chemical and powerful, always had been, or at least it had been since those childhood summers they spent at the college pool.

The air in the pub was thicker and hotter than it was outside; like in the old days, when it was filled with cigarette smoke. Fran ordered a pot of blackcurrant and lemonade and sat at a table at the far end of the lounge area, arranging her crossword and her legs until she looked relaxed, purposeful, and potentially attractive. She was not very good at *not* looking at the door. Every time she heard a noise, her head bobbed up. Is it him? Is he here?

From her table, she could see the convent hall out of one of the front windows. A dark BMW turned into the driveway at the side, and drove all the way to the back. Sister Mary Margaret had a visitor.

10.00 pm. She checked her phone. No new messages.

'Tequila,' Fran said to Pete.

'Coming right up,' he said.

By 10.30 pm, Fran had consumed four shots of Tequila and half a pot of beer; shunned Tricia Gallagher harder and stronger than she'd ever managed thirty years ago, and had given up on her crossword. She was certain she was far too attractive for a geek like Brian Ryan Junior anyway.

Bzzz. She felt it, she did, just where her pocket was.

Her phone wasn't even in her pocket, it was on the table. This place was making her crazy. She hated this town, she hated this pub. She hated Brian Ryan Junior. She picked up the phone to check it was still working. In the last 0.5 seconds, there were no new messages. 'Another one,' she yelled over to Pete, and as Pete walked to her table the door behind him opened. For a moment, she couldn't see who was coming, but it was surely him, thank God, please God, be The Captain.

It wasn't. It was The Boarder.

★ ★ ★

After the oval incident, Fran never wanted to see The Boarder again. When she realised she was pregnant, her resolve became stronger, and it wasn't hard. Soon as word spread, as well as her belly, The Boarder's parents removed him from the school in a clandestine Rolls-Royce moment that boarders and day boys and Mountain Sluts talked about for years.

Fran found out later that The Boarder's dad had driven to the ostrich farm a week earlier, where Gramps had signed a legal contract saying they could never ask for anything — money, contact, money, money. Gramps hated signing that contract as much as she hated that he signed it. Neither of them ever wanted anything from those scumbags. Parasites, Gramps said to her later, disappointed in himself. He shouldn't have been. All he'd done was make sure The Boarder was no longer in her life. He was irrelevant.

And yet she had imagined this moment thousands of times — daily at least for the first two years. Sometimes even now, in bed at night, she fantasised about seeing The Boarder. Somehow telling him to fuck off sent her straight to sleep.

Before she met Vincent, she fantasised that The Boarder would seek her out — walking home from Dante's kindergarten behind the convent, for example, or waiting in the playground at the primary school. He would beg her for two minutes of her time. He would tell her he was sorry he ignored her after the oval, and that he told his mates he fucked her three times when it was only once. He'd say sorry for neglecting to inform her about Tricia, as well as about his other sweetheart, who came with a lot of cattle. He'd beg for her forgiveness because she was so clever, so promising, and it was all his fault that she was a motherless single mother with embarrassing form-five results and no prospects whatsoever. He'd cry, he'd tell her he wanted to be involved with his son in any way possible. She would tell him to fuck off.

Nowadays, she always imagined a bar, just like this. She would see him first. She would approach him immediately, and tell him to fuck off.

He hadn't seen her, as far as she could tell. He

168

took a stool on the other side of the bar and ordered a whisky. He looked serious, unhappy. Women would find him attractive on Tinder, she thought, but not in the flesh. His hair was too blond for a man his age. He had absolutely no neck. Even when he put his chin up.

She turned the other way just in time. Phew.

Head down again, he wrote something on a piece of paper. Pete said something to him and they laughed. He continued writing.

Vows probably, for his wedding tomorrow. Whatever he was writing was intense — he rubbed his forehead, ordered another whisky. Could that Emily woman be his old sweetheart? Not likely. What was he writing that was making him scrunch his face like that — *You complete me?* You complete *meathead*.

Tricia Gallagher was taking the stool beside him. She was flicking her grey hair. She was sipping from her straw, saying something.

Fran couldn't hear the conversation, but so far it didn't look like there was much of one.

Tricia had probably just asked him how things are going. Whatever she'd said, it wasn't very exciting.

He had probably just said 'good thanks', seeing as how his lips moved but the rest of him didn't.

Tricia had probably just said: 'What's that you're writing', seeing as how she was pointing to the piece of paper he was still scribbling on, getting in his way.

The Boarder was probably telling Tricia to fuck off, because her face turned red and she stood up, her chair making a loud scraping noise that Fran found almost as irritating as the fact that people like Tricia Gallagher and The Boarder still existed.

It was time. It was the moment. She should get up, walk over, and deliver her line. But there must be something better to say than fuck off, which was very undramatic in the above Tricia scenario. She'd never managed to come up with anything, mind you, other than being indifferent, which was boring, never made a satisfying fantasy, never once sent her off to sleep.

She stood, head high, walked to the door, and pushed. She should have pulled. She was drunk. Her exit was not nonchalant.

It was even stuffier outside. She began walking towards the college — screw Father Frank, she'd walk through parish property if she wanted. She'd looked it up online and he was probably allowed to ban her under C843-1, which states that Catholics have the right to receive the sacraments when they a) have an opportunity to ask for them, b) are properly disposed, and c) are not prohibited by the law from receiving them. She was definitely not properly disposed. She breathed in through her nose and out through her mouth — *that's it, that's it*. She had no time for any of this nonsense. What with the physio for Gramps, and the fete, and Vonny, and the forecast — she had so much to do tomorrow and if she didn't hurry she would never get enough sleep.

'Collins?'

It was him, behind her. This was just like one

of her early fantasies, exactly here, exactly this.

She turned into the college driveway. The rambling buildings were empty, quiet, unlit. A spooky place for unwanted boys to spend their holidays.

'Collins!'

He was really calling her that, *Collins*. He probably never even knew her first name, and that it changed to 'Mountain Slut' forever because of him.

He was gaining on her. She was considering running. He grabbed her elbow.

Without thinking, she turned. 'Fuck off!' she said; the unexpected twist being that she also elbowed him in the stomach.

He doubled up, groaned.

'Sorry, shit, sorry,' she found herself saying.

'Jesus Christ, are you fucking crazy, woman?'

Yeah, she was, particularly now he'd spoken. 'Stop following me. Go away.'

'I will. I will. I just wanted to say one thing, it's important. I'm just asking for two minutes of your time.'

'One minute and fifty-eight seconds.' She showed him her phone — she had set the timer. She'd honed that line in one of her many fantasy threads. This was unnervingly real, and was about to get satisfying. So sorry, he was about to say. He was going to be so pathetic.

'There's not gonna be any trouble at the wedding is there?' he said, having retrieved half an inch of neck.

She did an hour's therapy a few years back, after someone on the tram told her off for having her foot on the seat. She got so angry and embarrassed that she jumped off the tram at the next stop and walked three kilometres along St Kilda Road. She was not the kind of person to put her foot on the seat!

Rest with your anger without reacting to it, the therapist said.

One minute and thirty seconds.

She rested with the heat in her head and the sting in her chest and the desire in her arms and legs to elbow this fuckwit in the stomach again, and then in the head.

'My fiancé's from Broady,' he said. 'The mother-in-law booked everything, nut job. I didn't have a clue, or a say, anyway. Plus I didn't think you'd still be here.'

She wasn't *still here*. But she had been resting with her anger for nearly three decades and she was sick of resting with it. She'd prefer to use it — for example, to get the information she wanted, craved, in bed alone at night. Where was The Boarder and what he was doing and what he was thinking and what he was feeling. This was her chance. 'So does the fiancé come with cattle?' Fran said.

'What? Ha! Like Cheryl Doherty, you mean? She didn't just come with cattle, she *was* one, fucking cow. She got custody, can you believe that?'

He was shining his torch on his wallet, where he kept some of the money that he made and some of the kids that he made. 'That's Tracy — she's thirteen, no hang on, fourteen. That's my Malcie.' He didn't venture a guess at his son's age. 'Don't see them as much as I'd like. Yeah, no, it's Emily tomorrow, second time lucky.' He closed his wallet, put it back in his pocket.

He was staring at her now, surely because he had shown her his, and was now expecting her to show him hers. She held the pause, offered nothing, even though she had hundreds of photos of Dante on her phone.

'So,' he said.

He would beg soon, adding the sorries, etcetera, he had hitherto neglected to say. After the grovels, snotty and teary, perhaps she could show him the one of Dante at his twenty-ninth at the Old Mill with his chef's hat on, or the video of him yabbying with Gramps at the old reservoir after his first day at school, using steak as bait for the exotic mud-water creatures. Dante hated school, loved yabbying.

'So,' The Boarder said. 'Will there be any trouble tomorrow?'

Rest with your desire to be violent, she said to herself, *Get used to the discomfort of wanting to kill him and it will pass.*

It worked this time. She looked at him, then at her timer, which was going off: two minutes and one second. 'There will be no trouble at your wedding,' she said, parting ways, indifferent, and in need of a new fantasy.

★ ★ ★

The headlights scared her; must have been on full beam. Fran did a netball dodge and hid

173

behind a tree, watching as Father Frank drove his BMW up the avenue, past the college, to the back of the church. Father Frank was returning from the convent, obviously, because it looked like the same car Fran had spotted when she was in the pub. He parked beside the vestry, the private room where priests played dress-up and other games. In the eighties, Father Alfonzo had played a lot of games in the vestry, before he was jailed.

Fran found herself running as close as she could to the vestry, and watching from an outbuilding. Father Frank was opening the boot, getting something out, impossible to tell what, and carrying it into the vestry.

She thought about running over to the boot while the priest was inside, but it was too risky. She wondered about breaking into the church later, but the priest might see her from the curtained windows of his horror-movie 1860s presbytery.

She had frightened him in confession that morning. He was moving his collection.

Fran made a decision. She would break into the convent via one of the windows in the women's toilets. One particular window was always open, had been since 1989.

27

Thirty Years before the fire

'Forgive me Father for I have sinned, it has been one month since my last confession and this is my sin. I had sex, last night.'

Fran had selected the 8.30 am as no-one she cared about ever went to the 8.30 am. Also, she'd heard a rumour that Father Frank was doing it this week. She'd heard a great many rumours concerning Father Frank: that he had decided to marry God rather than a beautiful girl from Brighton called Tina, for example; and that he had been offered a contract with the Bombers but had said no, again because of God; and that he was a good guy.

Fran couldn't imagine him landing a beautiful girl called Tina, and had never once seen him kick a ball, but he did seem like a good guy.

He arrived at the parish three years prior, fresh out of the seminary, twenty-seven years old, clean cut, 5'8", and massively into (talking about) sport, which got everyone on side immediately.

At first, the young priest followed The Mons around, looking like Robin next to an imposing Batman. Soon after, he graduated to being second chair to Father Alfonzo at the 10.30 Sunday mass.

Father Alfonzo was altogether less striking

than The Mons. He was middle-aged, no Italian olive in his pale-to-yellow skin. He had two extra chins, wore his belt below his sagging stomach and stuck the few streaks of hair remaining across his head using Vaseline. If he pointed his head at the sun long enough, it'd catch fire. When Father Alfonzo and Father Frank did mass together, they looked like they were a creepy uncle and his cute nephew.

During that period, Father Frank sometimes performed mass alone, but only in emergencies, like at Easter when there were simply too many services to service (although he would never have landed the Friday 3.00 pm gig, the biggy, the biggest, the grimmest of the year; when you had to stand in line and kiss Jesus's feet; and as well as eating Jesus meat you also had to drink Jesus blood. It went on for hours and hours. Afterwards, all the shops were closed, including the Servo and Gallagher's and even The Red Lion, and everyone was really down because Jesus had just died. The Mons always did that one, in a special dress.

Fran witnessed Father Frank perform his first funeral a year ago (another emergency, as there were an unprecedented number of burials that week, what with Chrissy and her mates careering into the Old Mill.) He was good, Fran thought. Everyone cried the right amount. The rumours were correct: he was a good guy. He was definitely ready to fly solo when Father Alfonzo 'left'.

Initial reports were that Father Alfonzo had 'left'/'moved north'/'moved sideways' because he 'needed some rest'. It was not long, however, before more information became available, and community discussions on the grandstand went more like this:

Father Alfonzo's been charged with touching up kids.

Father Alfonzo anally raped a seven-year-old altar boy in the vestry. His name is James and he's started speaking out.

Shh, we do not talk about these things.

Father Alfonzo is a paedo cunt and should burn in hell.

Shoulda known, shoulda fucking known, creepy pervert prick, fucking kill him, we should all fucking kill him, let's go, shall we go?

Oh come on, for goodness sake, we know nothing, leave poor Father Alfonzo alone.

Father Alfonzo masturbated a boarder in his bedroom in the presbytery. He and brother Colin took turns in the cinema room. Everyone knows what they're called, the boarders they abused — they're called the projector-room boys.

He's not even Italian, he just chose an Italian name, Alfonzo, I mean who the fuck would do that, choose a wog name, fucking paedo.

After Father Alfonzo 'left', young Father Frank took over the parish. Since then, everything had improved, including grandstand chat, which now went something like this:

Saw our PP without his dog collar again — what is he like?

He asked me to call him Frank.

I saw him swimming in the old reservoir.

177

He often has dinner with us.
Loves a good lamb chop.
You can tell him anything.

Fran was surprised, therefore, at Father Frank's response to her confession:

'You did WHAT?'

'I had sex, on the oval, at least I think that's what it was.' She waited, nothing. 'With a boarder.'

'You *think* it was the oval?'

'Ha, no, I think it was sex — as in — *ual* intercourse.' The curtain was closed, she couldn't see him without moving it, and she decided she'd better not.

His chair squeaked, then again. 'Did the boy insert his penis into your vagina?'

She was taken aback by his official language. 'Insert?' She was having a think. 'I s'pose that's what he did.'

'He put his erect penis into your vagina?'

She was also surprised by his sexual language, before quickly realising why he was interrogating her thus. 'Yes, then out again but not right out, in and out like that a few times, if you know what I mean . . . you might not.' Fran was not being obnoxious. She was actually recalling the strokes. She now understood that the young priest's questions were necessary; that her penance depended one hundred percent on the details.

'Brazen hussy; that's enough of that.'

She'd have to ask her dad about those words, they sounded old fashioned, but he'd probably involve the encyclopaedia and go into the Latin origins for ages. She'd do it herself. 'Brazen',

178

'hussy', remember to look those up. They probably weren't good, considering the priest's tone.

'Did you use contraception?'

'No,' Fran said. She wasn't worried about contraception. Her mum had taken ages to get pregnant the first time, and couldn't ever again. Fran was pretty sure she'd be barren and that an experience as shitty as the one she had could not possibly result in a child.

'Well, I suppose that's something at least,' said Father Frank. He paused again; his chair squeaked again.

Fran was wondering who'd be outside when she opened up — maybe The Boarder. She hoped she hadn't spoken loudly earlier. She hoped no-one had heard. Could anyone hear?

'Say ten Hail Mary's and ten Our Fathers,' said Father Frank, 'and I suggest you control yourself from now on and stay well away from boys.'

'That's going to be hard, Father. I'm starting at the college in two weeks, there's only twenty of us and there's five hundred of them.'

'Fifty Hail Mary's, twenty Our Fathers and . . . ' Fran didn't hear the last one. He'd slammed the shutter shut.

⋆ ⋆ ⋆

She was able to take Father Frank's advice for the following fourteen days. She stayed in the house, pretending she had a sore back, too scared to see anyone because they would all have heard by now that she was a 'shameless Lolita' (she had found the priest's slurs in her dictionary, and had also needed to look up 'Lolita'). Every hour, at least, she checked the mustard phone in the kitchen for the dial tone. It was working. There was no technical reason, this end, why Tricia Gallagher had not returned her calls.

She even refused to go with her dad to the city to get uniforms, and hence ended up with a summer dress that was four sizes too big and a blazer that was one size too small.

'You mean the girls are supposed to wear the dresses as short as that?' her dad said.

She was sobbing too hard to answer him. The blazer made the dress bunch up everywhere, and took away arm movement. Her dad couldn't sew. She couldn't sew. She was doomed, doomed.

Mrs Verity O'Leary 'popped by' the following day, and to everyone's surprise had her sewing machine and all her kit in the boot. Her dad must have told someone in town, and word got around. The dress was better, but Fran was still doomed, as she discovered on the first day of school.

★   ★   ★

She refused to take the short-cut along the fence on the Ryan side to the footy fields — which would take a relaxed ten minutes at most. She would arrive like everyone else, at the front entrance. Her father drove her, attempted to kiss her on the cheek, then left immediately as promised. 'You are not waiting and looking at me.'

She stood at the first oak of the avenue and took a breath. A new start. This was going to be amazing.

Tricia and the other form-five girls were in the quadrangle, and she realised too late that none of them were talking to her. She was standing in their circle and everyone was silent and looking the other way. After saying 'is everything okay?/this is weird/what's the matter?', and getting nothing back, Fran made her way to the assembly, holding back the tears as Father Frank and the new principal, Mr William Dickens, waxed lyrical about the college. Females had arrived. This was a new era, a fresh start.

Her first class was physics. She arrived early, and watched as boys filed into the room. It was almost full, and so far, she was the only girl. Fran was nauseous as she watched the door, and thought she might faint when The Boarder waltzed in.

'Hi,' she said as he walked past.

'Hi,' he said, taking a seat at the back.

'Is that the one?' she heard someone say, then some boys laughed and one of them decided on the nickname she would go by henceforth: 'Hey, Mountain Slut, meet me at the oval after school?'

'Ignore them.' The boy next to her had spoken. He was pretty and geeky, scratched his red arm all the time, didn't look like he belonged here. 'They're dicks. I'm Ollie.'

At recess, Ollie showed her his hiding places.

He'd been a boarder here since form one and knew everything. The new netball court was going to be great. 'If you're here taking shots, no-one'll necessarily know you haven't chosen to be alone. Plus, no man would be seen dead with a netball.' Neither of them looked natural at solo goal practice, but they could work on it. 'Lunchtime clubs are good too,' he said. 'Only victims go to clubs at lunchtime.'

She joined chess and badminton.

At lunch, she and Ollie talked under the grandstand. He made her promise to remember that they're all just abandoned and horny, and that that can make a lad crazy. She didn't see him for the rest of the day, and she was glad. It was even more depressing with him, somehow.

In biology, she counted the minutes till the bell. She had ordered her father to collect her, but now realised buses would be out front in the afternoon. Buses filled with boys and girls that might see her. When the bell finally rang, she walked as fast as she could to the grandstand, then along the paddock to her house, howling. Her life was over.

It wasn't, obviously. Not until May.

★ ★ ★

'Quiet, quiet boys and girls,' said Sister Mary Margaret, who was standing on the stage in the convent hall, addressing the pupils in front of her. There were at least eighty boys to the nun's left, and twelve girls to her right, including Fran and Tricia. The pupils had marched from the college to the convent hall in order to undertake their first co-ed dancing class.

'I have a very important announcement,' said the nun. 'Quiet, okay. The formal, as you know, is a week on Saturday, and I am very excited to let you know that we are going to be joined by top-quality girls from St Martin's in the Pines . . . '

Dozens of boys made raucous happy sounds. *The Micks from the Sticks. The Moles on the Poles.*

'Quiet! As well as the gentlemen from St Patrick's.'

A dozen girls made happy sounds. Apparently they were nice, the boys from St Patrick's in Ballarat. She'd heard the same.

'All of whom will be travelling a great distance, all the way from Ballarat, in buses, to join us. We must therefore impress them and will be practising every day until the dance. Are you ready? Girls, please take a seat.'

Fran and the other girls sat on the chairs at the side of the hall.

'Boys, please choose your partners.'

The other girls, who had not uttered a word to Fran for three months, had decided that today was the day they would change over to their winter uniforms. They all wore long tartan skirts, white shirts, blue jumpers, ties, and blazers. Fran was the only one with her legs showing, and the only one who was freezing cold. She had goose bumps on her legs. At the same time, her head was hot and her palms were sweating. The boys had formed a line, and were coming. Most would choose no-one as a dignified way out. For the rest it was first in, first served.

Where was Ollie? She needed Ollie. He wasn't here. He wasn't here.

As the boys walked past, many greeted her similarly: *Mountain Slut, three times by the lake, can I have a blow job, slut.*

She realised a lot of the other girls were getting it too; and that most had nicknames by now. Fiona was Pog (pig/dog), Maria was Truck (looks like one ran into you), Margherita was Greasy Wog.

The Boarder didn't say anything when he walked past all the way to Tricia Gallagher, who he pointed at — *up.*

Tricia had been chosen. She took The Boarder's hand and glanced at Fran. She was very pleased with herself, Tricia.

Thankfully, Rory McDonald had arrived. 'Would you do me the honour?' he said.

Everyone hated Rory because he was really bad at sport. Fran thought he was fun.

They were doing the Dashing White Sergeant. 'What's that?' said Rory.

'What?' The song ended; she was out of breath.

'On your dress.'

Fran looked down and saw that her uniform was wet. 'Weird, is there a leak?' She looked up at the ceiling, then realised everyone was staring at her.

She stepped back from Rory. There were two large round wet marks on her chest.

Her breasts were leaking.

She made it to the cubicle just in time.

'Are you okay?' Tricia Gallagher's first words since the Blue Light Disco.

'I'm fine.' She wasn't; and she wasn't able to vomit quietly.

'You can talk about it. Everyone saw,' Tricia said.

Fran rested her head against the side wall of the cubicle. She leaned into the bowl and vomited again.

'Francesca? I think we need to talk. Francesca!' Sister Mary Margaret was knocking on the toilet door.

There was a high window above the loo. She stood on the seat — it wasn't only unlocked; the handle was loose. She pushed with her head, careful not to scrape or squeeze her growing tummy as she edged her way out.

★ ★ ★

The puddles along Ryan's Lane were often icy in July. Fran took her time each morning, picking the best one: the roundest, the thinnest, the most transparent. She'd chosen well this morning. The lush winter grass looked even greener through it. She held the ice in her gloved hands and continued into town. It had melted, of course, by the time she reached the monument.

'Morning!'

It was Henry Gallagher; he scared her to death. He and his wife Shirley were doing some gardening at the foot of the tower. This route was safe this time of day. They had no business being here at 8.45 in the morning. Henry had a shrub, which he was planting in front of the photo of Ollie.

'So sad, this poor wee boy. Did you know him?' Mrs Shirley Gallagher asked.

'I did,' Fran said.

'You have to wonder what can lead to such despair,' said Henry.

Despair all right. Two months earlier, while Fran was escaping the toilet window, Ollie was on the lookout, taking forty paracetamol, drinking two bottles of whisky, then throwing himself off head first. He didn't leave a note.

'When are you due?' said Mrs Gallagher.

'Two months-ish.'

'You want a lift into town?'

'It's quicker to walk; thanks, though.'

'If there's ever anything we can do,' said Mrs Gallagher. 'I've got an old buggy.'

'Of course, great.' Fran wished people would stop shoving help in her face all the time. She upped her pace. She had exams looming. She needed to get a move on.

★   ★   ★

Fran studied alone in the living room of the convent. She'd pass fifth year, she would, then she'd never have to think about school again. The room was damp and dusty and cold, the open wood fire the only heating, and no-one ever lit it. Fran's only escape from this room was if

186

help was needed in the sick bay, or if she had an appointment there herself. Sister Mary Margaret, as well as being competent with music and dancing, was a nurse.

Today, Fran was required to help in the 'waiting room' (the kitchen) at the end of the day. None of the children was seriously ill and they therefore had too much energy for Sister Mary Margaret to bear. She had paperwork to finish, final medicines to dispense.

There were four of them today: a boarder who'd hurt his arm playing footy, a ten-year-old girl who had a bad headache, and Johnny, who was very particular with his cutouts, perhaps because he didn't have enough breath, or bugs, to do it over if he made a mistake. He looked impossibly sad for a seven-year-old.

'Are you worried about something?' Fran asked him.

'I am,' he whispered. He was very dramatic.

'What? You can tell me.'

'I don't like getting my photograph taken,' said Johnny.

Tears were in his eyes and Fran was immediately sad herself. This poor wee boy. 'That's not something you need to worry about,' she said, meaning it absolutely, and taking the spider he'd just cut out from a magazine. 'Whereas this spider!'

Johnny's eyes lit up. 'He's going on the lid.'

'He is not.' She helped him stick it on.

Sister Mary Margaret was calling for Johnny. The little boy gave Fran that sad look again and headed to the door.

'Ten minutes on the nebuliser and you'll be right as rain,' said the nun.

28

One Day before the Fire

The handle on the bathroom window was still broken. Not a coincidence: nothing parish-owned had been repaired for decades, also Fran always chose this cubicle, and had noticed the window at the Christmas fete.

She used her credit card to lever it open and dived in, not worrying about her stomach. She didn't mind that it was pitch-black, because she knew exactly where she was going: twelve steps to the door, right for seven, feel the wall on the left of the dance floor until reaching the door, and push.

She was in the corridor linking the hall to the convent. She brushed her hand along the wall as she walked, and when her fingers fell she took a breath. The inner hall was just as imposing when you couldn't see the Madonna and Ned Kelly eyeballing each other from opposite walls.

Subway tiles led her to the kitchen until she saw that the light was on. She couldn't hear anything, anyone. She pushed on the glass at the top of the kitchen door and entered the room.

The light above the sink was on, and the adjoining door to the sick bay ajar. She headed into the sick room, a wave of nausea hitting her. The same bed, the same bare space, the same blinds covering the window to the office next door.

She went into the office and opened the blinds above the desk, the same metal slats making the same clicking sound when separated, then boinging back into place.

If she didn't sit for a moment, she would faint. Perched on the orange tweed chair, she put her head between her legs and took two long breaths, returning upright when she was ready.

A large cabinet had been moved into the centre of the room. The hatch to the wine cellar was visible and open, and there was a light on down there.

The cellar was around ten by ten feet; three of its walls lined with at least ten shelves, on which there were dozens, and dozens, of treasure boxes. Most of the boxes on the right wall had been removed already, their varied shapes and sizes obvious from the dust that had once surrounded them.

Fran reached for the first one, a hatbox on the top left. It was covered in Barbie pictures. On the top was written *Adrienne, 3*. It was stuffed with photos of little Adrienne, in the sick bay with a bruised arm, dressed only in her pants. Fran put the box back, and took the next: *Allyn, 12,* who barracked for the Bombers and had broken his finger. She slammed the box shut when she saw a photo of little Allyn naked.

The boxes were in alphabetical order. She held her hand up as she looked at the photos, covering the things she did not want to see. There was Bernie, thirteen, a swimmer with shoulder issues, and there was diabetic Fiona and her big green eyes. She remembered Johnny, seven, whose ribs stuck out as he wheezed, his tongue between his teeth as he cut his precious insects. She lowered her hand. His ribs were sticking out in the photographs too, although she could not look at all of them. 'I don't like getting my photograph taken,' he had whispered to her.

K to Z had been moved already. Fran traced back from K slowly, from Kathy who liked chocolate, to Greg and his planes, to a shoebox that was too small to fit into its predecessor's dusty outline and which had no pictures on it.

Francesca, 15, was written on the top in green.

She slid to the floor with the box in her hand. After seeing the first picture, she covered the photos with her hand again, and looked only at the face of Francesca, fifteen, features ripe and with fear in her eyes.

The click of the blinds. She remembered the click of the blinds.

She was holding the last photograph in the pile, her palm covering the body, her finger stroking the face that was Francesca, aged fifteen.

'Francesca,' Fran said, crying. 'It's okay. It's gonna be okay.'

Her mobile rang: The Captain. She pressed End.

A door opened somewhere in the convent. She could hear the television — women yelling at each other, American women, screaming, *House-wives of New York.*

Footsteps. Fran put the photos back in the shoebox, and the box back on the shelf. She raced up the cellar stairs, into the kitchen, and out the back door, shutting it quietly behind her.

As she made her way across the oval, she saw headlights and heard gravel crunching on the convent's driveway. Father Frank was returning for the next load.

She didn't stop to recover at the top of the hill, and her legs were lead as she made her way down the monument track, the huge trees dark and deadly silent, her tears streaming, and her thoughts so loud as she sprinted along Ryan's Lane that they may have been coming out of her mouth: *Fuck you, fuck you,*

FUCK YOU.

PART FOUR

THE WATER TANK

29

The Day of the Fire

Fran called the local police station at 7.00 am. Detective Jeffrey McDonald, who had recently moved from Adelaide, was concerned and outraged and would investigate her allegations as soon as possible. Could she come in to the station tomorrow? It was mayhem today, he told her, what with staff shortages, the public holiday, the weather.

She could, she could. And it was good.

She would not think about it again until the cool change, and more importantly, until Vonny was safely back in the city. Tomorrow.

Today, she would survive.

The forecast had changed again, it might get to forty-three, and there were severe fire threats further north. Fran went over the fire plan with Gramps again at breakfast, but he only listened when she bribed him with lamingtons. Their property was the safest in the area. They would stay. Most disabled people would, she thought to herself, they'd have no choice. Who else in Ash Mountain would stay and defend no matter? she wondered; perhaps people with something to hide.

After breakfast, Fran was up a ladder clearing gutters and checking sprinklers. One of her Dad's seventies rock albums was playing on the

195

record player in the living room. The shutters on the outside of the windows were down, as were the canvas blinds she'd ordered and fitted around the edges of the veranda. She'd set up and filled two paddling pools, one by the swing chair under the blacked-out veranda, and one under the kitchen table. The inside windows and curtains were all closed. The house was full of fans, one in each corner, moving toast-crumb air every three seconds or so. The freezer was filled with ice and iced bottles and the fridge was filled with watermelon, bread, beetroot and beer. There were lemons and oranges in bowls on the table, as well as several empty bowls for ice. She'd fed and watered the elderly ostriches. She straightened the jackets and checked her emergency backpack — last used when Dante was bitten by a snake in South 1 in 1997, and regularly replenished since.

She was only halfway through the morning's jobs. Her energy was evaporating like the water she was hosing onto the tiled roof. 8.30 am. Thirty-two degrees. Fran had a large hat on, and white zinc cream on her nose (the only sun cream in the bathroom, and at least as old as the sherry and the Choo Choo bar). She was focused, fierce, and did not want to talk to The Captain.

He'd parked on the gravel, was taking something out of the boot and heading towards her.

She was on the top rung, gardening gloves on, a pile of gutter-tinder in one hand, streaming, water-wasting hose in the other. She should make her way down, but that would appear more welcoming than she wanted. Plus, the hose — he might tell on her. She was trying to hide it. It was not possible.

The Captain was carrying a basket filled with delicious-looking fruit and pastries. 'I've got a lot to apologise for. Got twenty minutes?'

She was wearing a pair of Dante's old footy shorts, and could not go down the ladder now.

The Captain seemed to sense that she was having some type of dilemma. He was having one of his own and — instead of looking up at her legs — chose to look in his basket. 'Make it ten and you can keep one of the jam jars.'

She threw the tinder and the hose to the ground, the latter hissing at his feet as she made a dash down the ladder.

'So sorry,' she said. The hose was alive, and was spraying his legs.

The Captain picked up the hose, pressed hard until the pressure was intense, and pointed it at her runners. 'No worries.'

She didn't budge, even as the hose moved up her leg, upwards again, leaving a line all the way to her neck.

'Did you say something?' she said, not flinching. 'I must be going deaf.' He was now spraying the hardest thinnest hose stream at her nostrils, eyes, ears and mouth. She could hardly talk. 'I see you've brought a selection of pastries,' she said.

⋆   ⋆   ⋆

197

Fran, dressed in Speedos and sarong, rocked on the swing-chair with an espresso cup in her hand. As she swung, she dipped her toes in and out of the paddling pool. The physio would be with Gramps a while yet. She was wondering about a second pastry.

The Captain, on the wicker chair opposite, still had his shoes and socks on, and was making a real mess of peeling a satsuma. He'd been ranting about The Boarder and his wedding party for ages. They'd kept him busy all yesterday, hence his no-show at the pub, for which he had apologised at least ten times. After the forecast came in, he'd informed The Boarder that the wedding was cancelled. And now this wind, and they're saying forty-three degrees! There'll be casualties by the hour. He had intended to take the family to the beach, get the hell out of here. The Boarder had threatened to sue, The Captain had sought advice, and the wedding was going ahead.

'He is such an arsehole.' The Captain had finally managed to peel the satsuma. He flicked his shoes off, it took a few shots, and dumped his feet in the pool. 'So our girls have fallen for each other, sweet,' he said, holding on to his deconstructed fruit. 'Fuck them,' he said. 'They're sixteen, they'll break up, they've known each other a week, they're idiots. Fuck the kids.'

Fran stopped her swing. She wasn't expecting that.

'I want to be around you,' he said, 'all the time.' He put the peel and its insides on the ground beside his chair. 'Can I come over tonight?'

'You can,' she said. 'Can you come over tomorrow too?'

'I can,' he said.

30

The Day of the Fire

ROSIE

Vonny is not gonna get these off me again. She tried at the pool Saturday, started lacing one up in the tent. She's so annoying. I cannot wait to see her. 'Back after the fete,' I say, kissing Dad on the cheek.

He's stressed. This wedding malarkey is one huge pain in the arse at the best of times but it's 205 degrees and all the guests are gonna end up in hospital, he reckons, not that he'd mind that happening to at least one of them. He's been on the phone to the Country Fire Authority, who've reassured him, and to Stephen Oh, who doubles up as a paramedic during busy periods. Stephen says he'll be on standby.

'You're catastrophising,' I tell him, then give him a hug cos that's what he needs when he feels like this. He's a simple creature, Dad. He puts an enormous hat on my head, gives me fifty dollars, and tells me to bring home a box of the best chocolates I can find and that the rest of the change is for me.

'They'll melt,' I tell him.

'Buy frozen peas too? And get back before the afternoon heat, yeah? I want you all near me today.'

I put my headphones on, choose the playlist Vonny sent me, and off I pedal into the fan oven.

*　*　*

The Collins house is a fortress outside, and cool and welcoming inside. Some song about it being '*time for a cool change*' is on. Vonny's mother is whistling while she undertakes an OCD tea ritual. Old Mr Collins is watching *The Love House* in his bedroom with Nurse Jen, and Vonny is already eyeing my Doc Martens.

'I'm not sure what to wear,' she says.

Don't do it, don't do it, Rosie, I say to myself.

The pause works. She goes for runners and sticks with her dungarees.

'This is good, Mum,' she says, looking at an Invasion Day poster she made. 'Is it for me? Can I take it to the fete?'

'Sure,' says her mother, resuming her whistling.

*　*　*

I take my boots off and carry them with me to the top of the ladder. I am not going to take my eyes off them even for one second. We get totally baked in the dinghy, but I don't forget my resolve, and have my Docs on again when we decide to head into town. Perhaps I'm being paranoid. Perhaps Vonny has stopped wanting to steal my shoes. I leave my bike at Dante's and we walk along Ryan's Lane, an earphone a piece so we can listen to Vonny's favourite new song,

201

which I'm not getting, but maybe that's just because I've never heard it before. I can't sing along like she is. She's dawdling too, she's such a city slicker.

★ ★ ★

Poor Mrs O'Leary, her Australia Day fete is a disaster. Even Tricia Gallagher only popped in for twenty minutes, she tells us. And she didn't even bother to muster decent spinning-wheel prizes — some second hand three-for-two books and a boogie board, for goodness sakes, here. There were supposed to be rides on the oval but they all cancelled yesterday.

Mrs O'Leary has a tight shirt on and there are large sweat marks under her arms and on her stomach. I believe she might have fainted had she not sat down in time.

Henry Gallagher has set up a cold-flannel area on his Lion's Club table. He dips one of his raggedy face-washers in a bowl of getting-warm water and then leans his head back and puts it on his forehead. There are drips coming down his face, but not for long. He's not sure this event is safe, he's saying. Even his hair is hot. His mind is mush. He's wondering if they should pack up.

Henry won't stop talking.

'The country's getting hotter and hotter. Have you seen the state of Lake Eildon? And what's the bloody PM up to? At the MCG in an air-conditioned VIP booth, holding hands with a billionaire coal miner.'

'I see you drank the Kool-Aid, mate,' says Marti Ercolini. 'Pack of death-cult hippies, what a load of . . . 'I'm so scared, it's Armageddon!' Have you forgotten that locust plague when we were nippers? Reckon I swallowed two hundred every time I went outside. But you were too scared to even come outside! What about the size of those hail stones at the swim meet in Castlemaine when we were in form four? Giant melons, they were. One of the buggers knocked Billy Fitzpatrick out just before he dived in for the four-hundred-metre backstroke.'

I can see it in Henry's eyes. He's really sick of listening to stupid people. So am I.

'And now all those wussies are finding new names for fires,' Marti is saying. '*Superfire, Megablaze, The Monster!* — as if this weather is something new. You remember the dust storm in eighty-three? Hazel McNamara died of asthma! And *Cyclone Fucking Tracy*, seventy-five, need I go on? Have you forgotten the summer when we had to drive to Lance Road to get water from the bore or else our kids would die of thirst? The year Billy Munro's eggs came out of his chooks ready boiled?'

Henry seems as keen as I am to move the conversation on. 'These bloody fans aren't making any difference.'

Mr Ercolini is suggesting they close at 2.00 pm, before the heat sets in, and that they take turns going to the supermarket in the meantime. 'It's the only air-conditioned public place in town,' he's saying. 'The freezer section will be mobbed with people pretending to need frozen peas.' Mr Ercolini says he wants to man the CFA stall for a while at least, especially on a day like today, and here's Pete Gallagher arriving with his Ash Mountain Football Club paraphernalia — 'Pete!'

The carnival isn't over, not yet. The people are mustering.

Mrs O'Leary will man the Ash Mountain Bottlers stand and is willing to give a fifty-percent discount for those who buy more than three bottles of any flavour including orange. She will also charge one dollar to hose people down for fifteen seconds under the awning out front, all proceeds going to a new town statue, as the one of Bert is a disgrace. Luckily, Pete Gallagher has not heard her say this.

Stephen Oh's arriving any minute, Mr Ercolini is saying. He's bringing the freezer from the servo, stuffed full.

Another prize could be getting a minute over the freezer, says Pete.

Or a free Sunny Boy, says Henry Gallagher.

Not likely, says Pete.

They've been discontinued anyway, says Mr Ercolini, Glugs and Raz's, can you believe it? What are we s'posed to do without our pyramids of ice?

Vonny has nabbed a table and is busy setting up her Invasion Day stuff, which includes her mouth, one poster and Spotify.

'Sharing information,' she explains to the Lions and the Footballers and the leader of the County Women's Association, all of whom are more than happy to help. Her stand, they all decide, should be between Pete's footy stand and Henry's Lion stand. That way, if anyone gives her hassle, they'll have Pete and Henry to contend with.

I'm not the only person who loves Vonny.

Mrs O'Leary just gave her a bitter lemon on the house. I'm a little huffy, period might be coming, or it could be this heat. I would love a bitter lemon for free. A sip would be good, even.

People start coming in, mostly because it's so horribly hot where they came from and they are all disappointed that it's even hotter here, that this is real.

A lot of people are going for Mrs Verity O'Leary's fifteen-second hosing, which is coming from the Gallagher dam, Mrs O'Leary explains, no need to tell. I reckon there may be need for antibiotics.

There are now twenty-one people in the hall, most in one item of clothing only, their grooming out the window for the day. At least half are at Vonny's stand because she is telling them stories that make it cooler. There's a song coming out of her phone, has been since she set up the table, a kind of lullaby, she explains. Every now and again she makes a sneezing noise and people laugh and some of them start to do it too, like Sister Mary Margaret, who's drunk, and Ned and Luca and Maz and Ciara, and even Pete Gallagher from the footy stand.

Choo!

I go outside for a reduced-price, fifteen-second hose and realise Mrs O'Leary has not considered the wet-T-shirt implications of her game. There are two dickhead boarders across the road. One has a Hugh Grant flop of hair and blubbering shoulders to match. The other is kicking random things, like the cigarette bin outside The Red Lion, which he has broken and does not care about because he is now looking at my nipples. 'Mountain Tits!'

'These are for women only,' I yell, and they scramble. But it doesn't feel good to have shocked Mrs O'Leary with two, or three, things at once.

I'm not bleeding, so there's no excuse for my mood.

Vonny is talking to a kid from my school and she doesn't look annoyed or even bored. I'm hungry, I eventually realise, so walk over and say, 'You want something from Ryan's?'

She wants a vegan salad box.

I tell her there are no vegan salad boxes at Ryan's.

She tells me she wants a roll and salad then, or a banana. This is Craig, she says.

I know, I say, Craig is the class arsehole, then I leave, stopping outside to pay Mrs O'Leary full price for a thirty-second hosing.

Ryan's is closed, and the supermarket is mobbed. There has just been some kind of incident in the world-foods section. Mrs Ercolini is on the floor under the rigatoni. The manager, Mohammed, is telling everyone to choose another aisle, so I do.

At the till, Giang tells me Mrs Ercolini isn't dead, it's just her ice cream melted and she slipped. I take my change and am about to open my backpack when I realise Vonny's brother is next in line.

'Hi Dante,' I say, packing my chocolates and my peas and Vonny's banana into my backpack.

'Rosie! Hey, have you seen the big V?'

'Yeah, she's at the fete,' I tell him.

'Changing the world?'

'The fete at least.'

'Is my mum there too?'

'No, she's at home, I think.'

Dante unties his ugly mutt and decides to walk back to the fete with me. I'm wanting so much from this encounter that I have gone silent. I want to know if I'm worthy. I want to know him — at least enough to be more comfortable than this. And I want to know all about Vonny, like, are there girls in the city who like her the way I do? I just bet there are lots.

By the time I have had a lengthy conversation in my mind, there is no time left. We have reached the convent hall. In my absence, the prizes have happened, and everyone is leaving and Mrs O'Leary is suggesting the committee pack up tomorrow and Dante is whispering something to Vonny.

He's wanting her help with an errand, she says. She doesn't say anything about me helping too, and neither does he.

'I've gotta go,' I say, giving Vonny a hard hug.

'I'll call you,' she says, but I bet she doesn't. I bet I spend the rest of the week checking. I should know better than to fall for a city girl.

At the monument, I stop and put the frozen peas on my face, and on my chest, and on my arms and legs. They get warm and squidgy really fast. It's better inside the monument, so I sit on the spiral stairs a while and check messages, Instagram, Facebook, Skype . . .

It's too hot to walk right now. I climb to the top and look around Ash Mountain. While the heat is eerie, like I am in another world, I recognise my town: the ostrich farm, McBean's Hill, the main street in the valley, the Gallagher farm and the Gallagher dam and the water tank. It's so beautiful here.

The chocolates are dripping out of my backpack, shit.

That's right, I have change! I put one dollar in the telescope and scan the town for Vonny, eventually locating her granddad's four-wheel-drive opposite the church. It costs me another dollar to see that she and Dante and Garibaldi are sitting in the front seat, watching a bride and groom getting their photos taken on the steps of St Michael's. Must be someone they know.

If only there wasn't a scorching two-kilometre walk before I'm sitting at the kitchen table with Dad and the girls, skulling a big, icy orange juice.

My money runs out when I'm looking at Ryan's Lane and I remember my bike. I left it at Dante's water tank. That's halfway, one kilometre. I can make it to his place no bother, I tell myself, then I'll be at the kitchen table in no time. I want lots of ice. I ring Dad to tell him.

'That's great honey, wedding party's arriving after photos but I'll be ducking in and out all night. Love you.'

'You too,' I say, promising to put on the hat he made me bring, and not lying.

It's a public holiday, so there are at least three cars out the front of each Shitbox, plus a boat every now and then. I'm starting to wonder about knocking on a random commuter's door and asking for a glass of water, but I don't know anyone in there, and they don't know me. It's another 200 metres to Dante's. I'm reconsidering the glass of water decision when my phone goes off.

It's Vonny, on video. She's in the four-wheel-drive. 'Sorry about running off. Dante wanted to check out his dad, he's the groom.' She points her camera at St Michael's. Women in hats and men in suits stand around confetti clumps, smiling at the sweaty bride and groom. A kilted bagpiper is squealing at everyone.

'Have I got a neck?' Dante is asking Vonny. He's sitting beside her, looking at himself in the rear-view mirror, his dog on his lap.

'Sometimes,' Vonny says to him. 'Where are you?' Vonny asks me.

'Almost at the water tank.' I show her the ground ahead. 'I'm imagining water. I'm starting to see things, mirages.'

Vonny is pointing the camera at Dante, who is now out of the car.

'Are you seeing what I'm seeing?' he's asking Vonny.

Vonny gets out and I see the sky on her screen and hear her say: 'Oh my God.'

Instead of lifting the brim of my hat, I watch Vonny. She keeps filming as she runs to the doors of St Michael's, yelling at people to get inside. But the doors are locked. She tells them to take cover, to find somewhere safe, and she tries to stop them but most of them head towards their cars.

The groom with no neck is still at the gates, yelling at Dante to stop causing trouble. What the hell does he think he's doing? There's a struggle. Dante punches the groom in the nose.

The town siren goes off and I stop looking at Vonny's screen. I lift my hat and look at the sky ahead of me.

'Rosie, take cover,' I hear Vonny say. 'Take cover, find somewhere safe. Gotta go, I need to ring Triple Zero.'

31

— *Triple Zero, what's your emergency?*

— Hello, my name's Veronica Collins, I'm just ringing because I can see a lot of smoke over Ash Mountain, like coming from behind the Ryan farm, on Ryan's Lane, I can feel it from here, it looks really big. That's the town siren, just gone off. I'm out the front of St Michael's Catholic church in North Road and there's like sparks, rolling in on the ground, and there's a whole stack of people from a wedding here. The church is locked, we can't get in there. The roads are chaos. Where should I tell people to go?

— *Triple Zero, what's your emergency?*

— There's been an assault. Some crazy bogan has just punched me in the nose; I'm gonna need the police and an ambulance and maybe some backup — there's an Aboriginal girl here stirring up shit as well. They're trying to get everyone to leave. I'm at St Michael's, Ash Mountain, it's my wedding. Please hurry.

— *Triple Zero, what's your emergency?*

— It's Tricia Gallagher, I've just heard the town siren. We're heading to the oval — just wanting to check that's still the right thing to do?

— *Triple Zero, what's your emergency?*

— Maz Montgomery here. We're about to get

into our bunker, McBean House on Ryan's Lane. So it's me, Ciara my partner, and our boys, Ned and Luca. We'll exit well before the hour runs out, sixty minutes, starting now. We've alerted our security but I want you to know too. Be good if someone's here.

— *Triple Zero, what's your emergency?*
— My name's Sam, I'm in the bathroom.

— *Triple Zero, what's your emergency?*
— We need help, we're in the bathroom.

— *Triple Zero, what's your emergency?*
— Thanks, it's fire. I'm Marti Ercolini. My address is thirty-three Dry Creek, Ash Mountain and I'm heading off now: me, my wife and my son-in-law, getting out of here. It's a big fire. It's coming in from the north-west and heading straight for the town, that's Ash Mountain. You need to let people know. Where were the warnings? Who the hell is in charge?

— *Triple Zero, what's your emergency?*
— Brian Ryan, Ryan's Lane. I may be needing some assistance. I'm in the farmhouse with the little ones, in the kitchen, under the table. Have you got any advice? Got it. I will . . . I will, thank you.

32

The Bunker

MAZ

Maz is reading *Katie Morag and the Big Boy Cousins* to Ned and Luca, and the cousins are being quite naughty. Ned and Luca are transfixed, particularly by their mummy's weird accents. It is eerily quiet outside. The timer on the wall says forty-five minutes and is ticking loudly. They will run out of air in three-quarters of an hour, and the fire hasn't come yet. Perhaps it won't, Maz is thinking, but as she turns the page they all hear an explosion.

'What's that?' Luca is trying to look at the glass hatch above their square chamber, which was blackness a moment ago and is now a rainbow of reds and oranges. And a fist, knocking.

Maz and Ciara turn their boys' heads away and cover their ears. They almost screwed up back there with Chook and Tricia; they will not turn around.

Maz is trying to read Katie Morag but she can't help it and looks. There's a boy knocking on the hatch. He has a plaster on his nose. There are two others with him, knocking:

Help, help us. Please, it's me. Let me in, let us in.

It's getting very hot, difficult to breathe, and the sky has changed colour and she can't hear a thing: that's right, she remembers, it's time to shut the hatch. Maz reaches up and closes it so the boys' faces disappear.

'Let's lie down, babies, let's lie face down for a few minutes. If we put our ears to the ground maybe we'll be able to hear someone talking in rainy old Leeds.'

The knocking may well have stopped, but Maz can't hear it now. Her face is pressed against concrete and the heat is unbearable and the noise is terrible and the clock is ticking and the boys are sobbing and so is Ciara because the bunker is shaking.

'It's the storm, honey bunches,' says Maz, holding three heads down with her arms, 'just the storm.'

The Red Lion

PETE

'Time to get inside,' Pete is yelling. A motley crew has been hosing and sprinkling, and stamping and filling buckets and wetting towels and sheets and blankets and cloths, but now it is time to retreat.

Everyone is in the bar but Pete and Lion Henry, who's hosing the roof. 'Get down now!' Pete yells, holding the ladder.

214

Henry isn't coming down fast enough. He's halfway when something hits him and catches his shorts. He stamps the flames with his hand, and he gets it, phew, but then he's hit in the socks and in the chest, again, and again.

Pete isn't sure if Henry explodes or if that's what it looks like to be on fire.

He is now inside the bar, and sliding the lock.

Pete takes a moment, unlocks the door again, and turns around.

There are fifteen people in the bar, and while they are all looking at him, it may be more to do with the fact that he is smoking, all of him, literally, and not because they all know he just tried to lock out a bushfire.

No-one is asking about Henry Gallagher either, not even his wife Shirley, who hasn't been spotted outside her house for decades, and yet is here on the floor and cradling a shaking lamb.

Sami and Perla are dousing Pete then shoving wet towels in the cracks of the door.

Mohammed and Craig are wetting the walls and windows with cloths.

Verity O'Leary is wanting to drown out the noise by putting money in the jukebox but the power is off and Giang from the supermarket is giving #CommuterKid from Shitboxville a free pot of blackcurrant and lemonade with ice because his #CommuterMum and #CommuterDad are busy filling buckets.

The Old Railtrack

DANTE

Dante didn't regret punching his father. The guy was going to die if he didn't get a move on. The church doors had been locked since the ceremony and, after many attempts to get in, everyone had fled. Against his advice, many had chosen their cars and turned south onto North Road, stopping soon after to remain there, some of them U-turning to head north and stopping soon after to remain there. There was no access in or out of the town and no-one could see a thing now, everything was smoke.

A few of the guests had chosen to take refuge in the adjacent presbytery but Dante was not into that decision and neither was Von. It was one huge pile of dried-out weatherboard tinder, that place.

The flames had reached the Ryan buildings; they were coming. He couldn't see anything except The Boarder, who he pulled from the ground.

'Get to the car,' he said to Vonny, who was with Emily the Bride, and the four of them ran across the road to the car, which was still parked opposite the first oak. Poor Garibaldi, he was shaking as Dante revved the engine. He sped along the nature strip, swerving to break through the fence across from the church.

'Where are we going?' The Bride in the back said, as if she wanted hashtags for the selfies she'd been taking only five minutes ago.

His mum had made him walk this route many times, so he knew it well. There were no buildings, hardly any trees. It was safe apart from the fire that was approaching from the north-west. The wheels hit the tracks, and Dante turned left, getting it wrong a few times before settling between the lines. They were now heading north-east, but not fast enough. He pressed the accelerator to the ground.

'What the fuck?!' The Bride said.

'What the fuck?!' The Boarder, his father, said.

Vonny knew where they were going. They should go off the tracks soon. 'There, we don't need eyes, that's it,' she said, 'slow down here and get off.'

Dante headed off the tracks and up the bare hill.

They were about to make it, so close, but the four-wheel-drive blew a tyre, swerved, and stopped halfway up the hill, the flames closer now, and coming straight for them.

'Okay guys,' Dante said, his dog tucked under his shirt and blanket, 'so we have to get out and run through the flames to a burnt area — in that direction.' He pointed at the oncoming fire. 'It'll feel wrong but if you cover yourself and bolt, it's not. As fast as you can. It's the end of the line, it's thin, we can do it. There are blankets behind the chairs, got them?'

They had one each.

'Are you ready Von?'

'Aha,' Vonny said, turning to The Bride in the back, and noticing her heels, shit. There were no spare shoes in the car. She grabbed her veil and pulled it off. 'You ready?'

'Yeah,' said The Bride.

Then to The Boarder: 'You?'

'Okay.'

The four of them grabbed a door handle each.

'On the count of three,' said Dante.

McBean House

BOARDER #3

'Dyke bitches,' Boarder #3 is saying. He and his best mates, Boarders #1 and #2, have just sprinted from the bunker to the house.

Boarder #1 is there first, and opens the shutters enough to slide the glass window, so the three of them can crawl inside.

There are embers on the living-room floorboards. Boarder #3 is slapping them with his thong while Boarder #1 is opening the outside shutter and closing the glass.

Boarder #2 unplugs his earphone and the song he's listening to plays from his phone: 'The Ballroom Blitz'.

The shutter has now reached the top. The trio stand in line at the glass windows, mesmerised by the view. Flashes of red and orange and yellow colour the sky and their eyes. Several fires are interacting up there.

Boarder #1 can't take his eyes off the big one at the back, which joins forces with the others and it's on.

Embers are shooting at the house, pounding the glass.

The boys find each other's hands, and take another step back.

The Water Tank

ROSIE

Flip forward if you must, but my death will be much more satisfying if you don't. Won't be long, promise.

That's right, it's me, Rosie, in the water tank. Dad just called me, thank God. He's on speakerphone and his words are echoing.

'Tell me about the fete.'

I can't hide it. I'm finding it hard to think about the fete, I keep flipping forward to now, but who can blame me.

'So we're all playing a game,' Dad tells me; he says he and the girls are under the kitchen table playing I-spy. Cathy's spying something beginning with L, and Amy is guessing leg but not whose or which leg, so she's specifying your leg, which is correct, but no-one is giggling.

'So I had the perfect day,' I say. 'Imagine, in this heat. I won on the spinning wheel, Cathy, free highlights at the Palm Tree Unisex Hairdressing Salon, we could go together. And Vonny taught us all a song that's from a lost Aboriginal language, Inanay, you can never even try to know what it might mean.'

I can hear that Harriet is spying smoke and

219

that Amy is spying something hitting the windows and that Cathy is too hot to spy and is saying Our Father who art in Heaven Hallowed be Thy Name.

'How much water is in there, baby?' Dad says.

I lean out of the deflating dinghy, and put my finger in the simmering water. It hurts but I don't want him to know. 'Dunno.'

'You should maybe get out of there? Make a run for it? Head for the house?'

His voice is quivering and the kids are crying and it's noisy where they are. He knows I am going to die and that he is too, and that so is Cathy and so are Amy and Harriet and all I can think to say is, 'I love you.'

'You're so resourceful, baby girl. I love you.'

The phone is dead.

★ ★ ★

I don't have long to be resourceful, and I am not good at it till the very end, as you will see. The water is boiling now, the sky is roaring, and there is nothing to paddle with but my arms, which I decide against because the dinghy is melting anyway. I sacrifice feet and calves and get into the bubbly water. I scream a lot. I'm not brave, but I make it the three steps needed so I can take hold of the smouldering ladder with my hands.

Oil rags are firing at me from above and I can no longer feel my legs or hands and the heat no longer feels like heat. I am yelling a lot and have only made it one third of the way up the ladder. I can't go any further, my hands may even be stuck, and my feet, why did I take my shoes off. Another missile. They are attacking from above, landing in the water, landing in the dinghy, knocking Dante's Esky off its ledge, landing in my hair. I scrape a hand off a rung, grab the piece of burning bark in my hair and throw it into the tank. It works.

Dante's stash is on fire.

I fall back and land in the deflated dinghy. I have probably broken bones already, but not my nose, it's above water. I inhale the weed and the other smoke as hard as I can, which isn't very. There is a circle of black above me, black and red.

You've caught up. It's happening, now, and while I may be resourceful, it's still the worst death imaginable.

PART FIVE

THE TREE

33

The Day of the Fire

MAZ

It takes a long time for Maz to open her eyes and even longer to lift her head. She watches the clock. Thirty seconds to go. When it reaches ten seconds, she flinches, waits another one, two, three, four, and then opens the hatch to a smoky outside.

Ciara and the boys, who have been lifeless on the ground, begin to cough.

'Adventure's over,' Maz says, guiding Ciara up the ladder first, and then Ned and Luca, until they are all standing outside the opening to their bunker, looking at the new world.

Everything in Ryan's Lane is burning or burnt: the shearing shed, the Ryan farmhouse and outbuildings, the Collins house, The Shed of the Dead, Dante's shack, and Dante's water tank, which is bending, falling over, spilling, gone.

Everything is gone, except McBean House, which the fire has shunned by some miracle. It has not been harmed. Not only that, but three boys are opening the glass door and coming outside.

The two groups face each other, unable to move for a moment, until Maz runs towards

225

Boarders #1, #2, and #3 and says: 'I'm sorry boys, I'm sorry. Are you okay?'

She hugs them, and they are all allowed to cry at last.

34

'Slugs are the first to emerge after a fire.' Gramps had read this to Fran from the *Encyclopaedia Britannica* once, under B, if she recalled correctly. She'd asked why the town was called Ash Mountain and he'd asked for M for mountain ash, E for eucalyptus, and B for bushfire. Her arms were sore and she was bored by the time he said: 'Nothing in here, very disappointing. I should write to the editor.' He then showed her a picture of a slug. 'See these little guys? They come out of the smouldering ashes, and they're, like, 'Yeah, hi, what's up.''

But Gramps was wrong. The first to emerge were not slugs but humans. Like Fran, who'd crawled out of the monument and made it to the ghostly hall, which had been abandoned mid-fete. The spinning wheel had stopped at Lose a Turn. The Best Knitted Cat had gone to Lena Kamiński.

It had been dark in the hall, as if it was night, except every now and again the windows became red. Outside, objects were exploding and firing at the building. Fran had realised she was standing, frozen, in the middle of the dance floor, the stalls of her community surrounding her — Lions, footballers, netballers and Invasion Day posters taking turns to be illuminated by the blasts from outdoors.

Invasion Day. Vonny had been here.

A window smashed. Fran had run to the toilets, no-one there. She ran back into the hall, and through the connecting corridor into the foyer of the convent. 'Is anyone here?' she yelled. 'Sister Mary Margaret?'

She ran along the thin hall to the kitchen, which was empty too. Then into the sick room, then into the office, kneeling to look under the cabinet. There was no lock on the hatch. 'Vonny? Are you there?' She opened it, but there was no-one, and nothing, in the wine cellar either.

Fran had found Sister Mary Margaret in the cold downstairs living room where she'd studied in fifth year. The nun had finished two casks of rosé, was wearing a hippy retro maxi dress, which she'd peed in, and was unconscious on the sofa. Fran had to carry her out, and she made it just in time.

The convent was now on fire.

She staggered her way along North Road, trying not to look at the burning outlines of the places she used to know inside and out; and trying not to look at the nun, the bony woman she was carrying. Where were the emergency services? There had to be somewhere safe, a building that was not on fire.

She tripped, perhaps a ladder, and thought better than to check what it was. She had reached the pub, and it had survived, so far. She opened the door, and deposited the nun on the slate floor.

★   ★   ★

228

The notice board, which had held the same printed sheet re Friday karaoke for the last few years, now had a new purpose. Verity O'Leary had a notepad in her bag, so people could write the names of their loved ones on it. She was saying a prayer and kissing each one before posting it on the board.

Pete was in his 'firey' gear, but it wasn't safe to go outside yet. He was waiting for directions.

Nurse Jen had gathered a phone from each network, and was charging and trying each on repeat. She had put her grandson, Berty, six, in charge of the landline. He was looking at the timer on one of his gran's borrowed phones: *58, 59, 60, beep beep beep.* Time to look. The little boy picked up the handset and listened, everyone in the room staring at him. 'Nup,' he said, setting the timer to zero again.

There were dogs and cats everywhere. Someone was holding a kangaroo. Someone else was holding a sheep.

Outside, the defence team was hard at it. The building wasn't safe, not even close. There were men and women on the roof, men and women on the ground all round, and no sign of help.

Not slugs, but humans, creeping out all over the place: cracking, scraping their way from the smoking ash, with an insatiable need to help.

'Have you seen Vonny?' Nurse Jen was checking Fran over, bandaging her hand. 'Is Vonny here? Has anyone seen my daughter?'

'I saw her at the fete,' said Verity O'Leary, who was comforting the commuter kid — who was wanting a shot on the big phone.

'What time?'

'Everyone left about two, so two.'

'Vonny and Dante drove to the church,' said Sami, 'in your dad's car.'

'Dante?' No, he was supposed to be at the beach with his girlfriend.

'We saw them around three, parked opposite the first big oak,' said Boarder #6, who was the one holding the kangaroo.

'When everyone was coming out,' said Boarder #8, whose arm was around Boarder #6.

'Of the church,' said Boarder #7, arms crossed.

⋆ ⋆ ⋆

Fran ran out into the darkness and was stopped by the smoke. She couldn't see the door behind her anymore. Which way to St Michael's?

Ash was snowing all around her, and Fran was thinking, *Vonny isn't in the water tank.* She stopped herself falling to the ground. She'd wished for this, after all, if only for a little while. Vonny was not boiling steaming screaming dying dead in the water tank.

It was Bri's little girl. Rosie. Rosie had worn the cherry-red Doc Martens today.

Fran wanted to fall, she wanted to cry.

But she couldn't, because *her* little girl, Vonny, could still be alive.

And her son. She should have known Dante would come back to take a look at his father, she should have known.

Which way was the church? She must have

turned around too many times. She was dizzy. Nothing was the same. Everything was burning.

That way, that way to the church. She had spotted the pub again. She walked carefully, one step at a time, checking out each car as she made her way north on North Road.

Sedan: no-one in the front seats; metal safe intact in the back seat.

Hatchback: driver only, not burnt on the outside, but probably on the in; photo albums melted into the passenger seat, back window open, two dog bowls in the back.

Audi, BMW and Toyota: with only a driver in each; all three of them dead Ercolinis.

Soft-top, hatchback, ute, ute, sedan: no humans — they must have bolted — just the things they chose to save.

No four-wheel drive, not yet.

The line of trees to her left was ablaze, including the oak opposite the spot where her children had last been seen. The car wasn't there. The college buildings were on fire and when she heard something crash in the distance she realised the grandstand had fallen. Behind that was the ostrich farm. Her house, the safest in the shire, was ablaze, and that's when she knew her dad hadn't made it. As was Dante's shack across the road, as was every building on the Ryan farm. The water tank wasn't in the sky anymore, it had gone too. Nothing could have survived over there.

She continued to scour vehicles on the main road: *Volvo with wedding-hatted guests and their overnight bags; Ford with a couple and wrapped present in the shape of a toaster; van with tools; four-wheel drive with boat.*

The presbytery was on fire, but the bluestone church seemed safe. She pushed the doors, but they wouldn't budge. She knocked on the doors. 'Dante? Vonny? Is anyone in there?'

She ran around the side of the church. The presbytery next door was beginning to slump, burning pieces of it rocketing towards the church and vestry. Red branches were falling from the trees, embers were flying.

Father Frank's BMW was parked at the door to the vestry, boot open. The vestry door was ajar, and a spark had caught one of the purple gowns on the hooks in the corner. The priest was in his black-and-collar on the floor, dumping the contents of his treasure boxes into bin bags, then discarding the colourful cases in a bonfire beside the door. He'd filled two bags so far, and had at least another two to go. If he'd seen Fran, he hadn't let on.

'Father, have you seen Vonny?' She was beside the bonfire, at the door.

'It's you.' She startled him momentarily. Then he continued emptying photographs into a bin bag. 'Don't think so.'

'This is what you're doing, Father? This is what you're saving? Have you seen Veronica, or Dante? Is anyone in the church? Why is it locked?'

He paused as he took in one of his pictures, distraught that this was happening to him. 'It was safer for everyone to get out of here,' he said.

So he had locked the church himself.

232

He grabbed the two bin bags he'd filled, barged past her and the small fire, and tossed them into the boot of his BMW. Could she not see that he was very busy?

On the way back in, flames caught his leg. The pain was making it difficult for him to empty the boxes and fill the bags, but he was determined.

She could grab him by the hair and drag him out now, and it would be a good idea because all the dress-ups in the corner had caught fire.

She could, she could drag him out, but she decided against it.

He was cry-praying while he emptied and filled, but it didn't seem like he was talking to God.

She could persuade him with words about the Bible and heaven, and probably should now, because the bag he was filling had caught fire and so had his hair, as well as nearly all the empty treasure boxes, which were in flames and blocking the door. But she decided against it.

A branch landed close to Fran, and the presbytery collapsed behind her — something in that burning house was squealing. She decided not to look.

'You've got to get out now, Father,' she said. 'The pub's safe, come with me, we'll go there. Look at what's going on around you, forget about all this.' She pointed to the photos.

Fran dodged another branch just in time. It was now blocking the door to the vestry.

'Father?' She held her hand. If he took it, he'd get out. He'd be safe.

He didn't take it. He was still busy.

A photo floated before her. She didn't mean to catch it.

Ollie, eleven, who had eczema, on the arms especially.

Ollie, her friend under the grandstand. Ollie, who tossed himself off the monument. Ollie.

The priest, now realising the severity of his situation, was trying to get out. He was looking for her help, had his hand out. She may have taken it had he not tossed a loaded bag out with his other arm.

She caught it without meaning to, and immediately tossed it back at him, which made him lose his balance and stumble back.

She grabbed one of the bags he'd put in the boot and — as he got up again — pushed it against his torso. He fell back into the pile of smouldering photographs. She threw the bag on top of him, took the second bin bag out of the boot and tossed that in too, collecting the photos that had leaked in transit without looking at them, adding them to the inferno, before kissing the one of her friend Ollie and throwing it in last.

35

There was no point getting in the BMW. The road was jammed, and she didn't need to. The vestry and church and presbytery were now so bright they showed her North Road, and the broken fence across from it. She knew where to go. She put her blanket over her, and ran.

She recognised the slope of the hill leading down to the old railway line, but was only looking at her feet, one at a time. She had to zig-zag to miss burning debris and several dead birds and animals, and almost fell when she reached the railway tracks. She turned left, seeing nothing but the trail ahead. The fire had passed through here already, leaving the dark-grey, smouldering clearing that surrounded her.

She could see the hill now. Soon she would spot The Tree clinging to its side, and the Old Reservoir tucked in beside it.

That was it, The Tree.

No, it was another one, just to the right of the tracks. A car had crashed into it.

She ran.

And could now see that it was a four-wheel drive.

And that there were two figures inside, sitting upright.

And that they were black. Burnt.

She opened a door, and one of the bodies fell

out, breaking to dust before her.

Fran fell to the ground and yelled.

She would never get up.

★ ★ ★

'Mum?'

Vonny, it was Vonny, she was holding a water bottle to her mouth.

'Mum?' It was Dante, going through her backpack, putting another blanket over her. 'We're okay, that's not us, that was the back door you opened, those two chickened out, they didn't get out of the car, it's not us, we're here, we ran right through, right through, me and Von are here.' Dante was crying. 'Don't stand up,' he said. 'Don't look, no need to look. Stay still, we're going to carry you up to the water.'

She could walk, she said, but this wasn't true. Her children carried her to The Tree, and all the way down to the water, where Dante's dog, Garibaldi, was having a drink. The reservoir was no more than a puddle now, but enough for them to lie in. They did this, side by side, looking up at the dark-grey sky, silent until a helicopter flew over, then another, another, some with water to dump, some with news.

Oh God, what would the news be?

Sirens began to wail, lights took over the smoke.

The city was here.

In the corner of her eye, Fran saw Dame Miriam McDonald. The aged ostrich was approaching the other side of the reservoir, taking nonchalant crunchy steps towards the water, and bending for a sip.

The three of them were half submerged in muddy grime, sobbing, looking up at the firework sky, silent, but Fran was already making plans.

The three of them were okay.

Her hand was burnt but it was bandaged and it didn't feel sore.

Dante was perfect, physically, Vonny too.

So they should get up. They should have some more water, walk back to town, head for the fire trucks. They should get gear on, they should help.

Fran was about to sit up when Vonny, still sobbing, squeezed her hand and said — 'What are we supposed to do now?'

Her girl had asked her the exact same thing she'd asked her father — in this very place, dressed in black, all those years ago.

She was so glad she had an answer.

Acknowledgements

I finished the first draft of this book in November 2019, and sent it off to my brilliant agent (Phil Patterson, thank you!). I'd been working on it for nearly two years, and it hadn't been easy living with me. My husband, Serge, my grown-up children — Anna and Joe — and my sister, Ria, all suffered. Thank you so much for listening to me go on about it, for reading it, and for not judging me for having my earphones in all the time.

Thanks Maz, for reading this, and for being Maz.

Thanks to Mum and Dad, who made a beautiful home for us in the country.

And to my town, bushfire territory.

The manuscript came back for me to edit when the 2019–2020 fires were under way. A photo that shook me appeared on my Facebook page (thanks Sharon Kelly!). My brave, tireless and amazing publisher, Karen Sullivan (thank you!) tracked down the photographer — Robert Dixon, from Port Macquarie. He'd taken the photo of his daughter Ava, and was happy for us to use it for the cover. Thanks so much for this amazing photo, Robert. Ava is a star.

Thanks to Brendan, who I found on the Mallacoota hashtag on New Year's Eve. He was the only person getting information out of the town, and his tweets were both poetic and horrific. He described the firestorm as it came in, and also his behaviour, step by step. His story is the most gripping and haunting I've ever heard.

And thank you to Felicity McCreadie, who's been keeping me informed while driving huge trucks of supplies from Melbourne to her town of Corryong, rallying support and donations. You're amazing, Fliss. (Go The Moles on the Poles)!

I could never have imagined stories as heroic and traumatic as the real ones I'm hearing now — the fireys, the farmers, the animals, the heroism, the kindness, the grief, the anger, the determination . . . the animals. Lives interrupted, changed forever, the disaster only just beginning.

Thank you to everyone who helped me get this out of my system.

Cover Image
Photographer's Note

My name is Rob Dixon. I'm a father of four kids living in Port Macquarie, a town on the Mid North Coast of Australia. The 8th November 2019 was a pretty intense day for us. Bushfires had been raging around the town for almost two weeks. Firefighters were doing their best to contain them, but they just kept burning. It was hot, dry and windy. People and homes were under threat. Animals were dying. It was scary.

As I drove to pick up my kids from school that afternoon, it was clear the situation had now become a lot more dangerous than I'd thought. The fire was closer, the smoke was choking and the sky was an eerie red colour — looked like I was on an alien planet.

We arrived home and my sons immediately ran out into the backyard to look at the sky and try to catch some of the ash that was floating down. Back inside, I stood at the end of the hallway, looking toward the open front door. An intense orange glow filled the doorway.

As I watched, almost mesmerised, my daughter walked out of her room, up the hall, and stood in the doorway.

The image in front of me was amazing. I just had to capture it.

I quickly grabbed my phone from my pocket

and went down on one knee.

'Looks so weird, Dad,' my daughter said.

'Sure does, sweetheart,' I replied.

Click. I took the shot.

She silently stood there for a moment, then, quick as a flash, took off into the yard.

Thankfully the fires didn't affect our particular part of town, but other surrounding areas were hit badly. The Australian bushfires are an awful thing and the 2019 season was a particularly devastating one. Hundreds of homes and wildlife destroyed. Thousands of hectares wiped out. Many lives lost.

The photo of my daughter is a stark reminder of that day.

I'll never forget it.

— *Rob Dixon*

Other titles published by Ulverscroft:

WORST CASE SCENARIO

Helen FitzGerald

Mary Shields is a moody, acerbic Glaswegian probation officer. Foul-mouthed and kind-hearted, she's one of the best; but it's hard to like the unrepentant clients who have done terrible things, and one day she's going to get fed up and take things a step too far . . . Liam Macdowall is that step too far. Imprisoned for murdering his wife, he's published a series of letters to her in a book that makes him an unlikely hero — and a poster boy for men's rights activists. Liam is released on licence into Mary's care, but things are far from simple. Mary develops a poisonous obsession with Liam and his world, and when her son and Liam's daughter form a relationship, Mary will stop at nothing to impose her own brand of justice . . . with devastating consequences.

THE CRY

Helen FitzGerald

When a baby goes missing on a lonely roadside in Australia, it sets off a police investigation that will become a media sensation and dinner-table talk across the world. Lies, rumours and guilt snowball, causing the parents, Joanna and Alistair, to slowly turn against each other. Finally Joanna starts thinking the unthinkable: could the truth be even more terrible than she suspected? And what will it take to make things right?

VIRAL

Helen FitzGerald

Leah and her adopted sister Su are almost the same age, but have always been opposites. Leah is wild and often angry, whereas Su is successful and swotty. When they go on holiday together to Magaluf to celebrate their exam results, it is Leah who their mother worries about — but it's Su who doesn't come home. Su is on the run, humiliated and afraid: there is an online video of her drunkenly performing multiple sex acts in a nightclub. And everyone has seen it. Their mother Ruth, a court judge, is furious — but also searching for a way to bring Su back when she doesn't want to be found . . .

THE DONOR

Helen FitzGerald

Just after her sixteenth birthday, Will's daughter, Georgie, suffers kidney failure. She needs a transplant, but her type is rare. Will, a single dad who's given up everything to raise his twin girls, offers to be a donor. Then his other daughter, Kay, gets sick. She's just as precious, her kidney type just as rare. Time is critical, and Will has to make a decision. Should he try to buy a kidney? Should he save just one child? If so, which one? Should he sacrifice himself? Or is there a fourth solution — one so terrible it has never even crossed his mind?